# Would you like a FREE e-BOOK?

Got to my Author Website (below) to download your **FREE** copy of ***Skins Game, and other short fiction***

A baker's dozen of Phil Truman's short stories in a range of genres from humor to horror. Guaranteed to deliver a laugh and make you shed a tear.

A no-obligation, absolutely FREE offer.

http://www.philtrumanink.com

# West of the Dead Line

The Dead Line, as it came to be called, was a railroad—the Missouri, Kansas, and Texas—cutting across the middle of Indian Territory. It ran straight south from Caldwell, Kansas to Fort Reno, I.T., then down through the Cheyenne and Comanche and Kiowa lands, crossing the Red River into Bowie, Texas. It was a line on the map, a demarcation. West of it no law existed, only outlaws. On trails out there, notes put up on trees and posts, sort of reverse wanted posters, let lawmen know they'd be killed if they continued their pursuits west of the Dead Line.

Throughout the 225-year history of the U.S. Marshals Service, over 200 deputies have been killed in the line of duty. More than 120 of those lost their lives in the Indian and Oklahoma Territories between 1850 and Oklahoma statehood in 1907.

In the storied times of the American West, no place came close to matching the dangers and mortality these federal officers faced doing their jobs. Their courage, resolve, and dedication to duty were beyond reproach . . . or the most part. Those who survived became titans in the legends of the West, particularly one man called Bass Reeves. These stories are fiction, but the encounters this lawman faced, and The Dead Line, were not.

# West of the Dead Line
## Tales of an Indian Territory Lawman

Phil Truman

Publishing

PTI Publishing
Broken Arrow, OK 74012

*For the gang I ride with: the Cherokees Dangerous Bob and Back-Shooter Bill, the Cajun Thibodeaux Rix, the Choctaw Grif Bad Horse*

# Bringing in Pike Cudgo

From an interview with Jud Coldstone of the Creek Nation—posseman, guard, and cook to U.S. Deputy Marshals of the U.S. Court for the Western District of Arkansas:

*Ever tribe in the Indin Ter'tory had they own police force, which come to be known as the Lighthorse Police. Most these was well thought of for the work they done and the peace they kept, but treaties did not allow them to arrest outlaws who was not citizens in their nations. That sit'chashun attracted some of the worst outlaws in the West to take up livin' permanent in the Indin Ter'tory. It were left to the federal court in Fort Smith, Arkansas, presided over by Judge Isaac Charles Parker, to arrest any white or colored man in the Ter'tory who done crimes again Indins, or any Indin who done crimes again white or colored men; leastways, any who the Indins didn't never claim as citizens. They was some negros in the Nations knowed as freedmen who come there after Mister Lincoln declared them emanstipated from being slaves. I oncest read where, back in '88, the federal gummint figured that twenty thousand white people and freedmen lived in Indin Ter'tory, and out of them, mebbe one fourth was law-'bidin'. Out of ever ten men convicted in Judge Parker's court, seven was white, three was colored, and one was Indin.*

*There weren't no other court in the country quite like Parker's. Not likely the country will ever see 'nother court like that, or the kind of lawmen who served it; going out into the Ter'tory t'bring in them outlaws to stand trial like they done. They was an exceptional brand of men, them deputies, especially one such former slave named Bass Reeves.*

Deputy Marshal Bynum P. Nelson felt surprise right before he died. He had a fraction of a second to be pissed, but he was mostly surprised. It never occurred to him that Pike Cudgo would walk right up to him, and stick that eight inch blade into the left side of his neck. He knew the Seminole freedman was a mean and dangerous sumbitch, but he'd been caught off-guard by Cudgo's cordiality. It was his last mistake.

"You Deputy Nelson?" the man asked. He came walking up to him out of the night shadows right there on the main street of Waurika, smiling like they were at a church social, and he was about to introduce himself. "Your man, Maha, said you's lookin' for me."

He started to stick his hand out as if to offer a handshake, slid a bone-handled Boulder knife out of his coat sleeve and stabbed it into Nelson's neck, right between two vertebrae, severing the lawman's spinal cord. The surprise came up in Nelson's brain the second he caught a glint of the raised blade, but that split-second was all he had as the emotion died right along with the rest of him that fatal instant there on the night streets of Waurika, I.T. in 1889.

Cudgo embraced the slumping body of Nelson while he jerked the knife out of the lawman's neck, let the dead weight of him drop to the dirt street. Cudgo wiped the blade on a faded red bandana that hung from his belt, standing there looking around. Cruel black eyes searched for anyone watching; anyone he thought might care about what he'd just done, anyone else he might have to take care of. The mean black face expressed a mask of cold-blooded dispassion. Human life had no value to Pike Cudgo, just his own.

Nelson's posseman, Barna Maha, himself a Seminole, had told the deputy he knew where Cudgo had holed-up, thought he could ride out there and talk the outlaw into giving up. Said he thought it'd be better if he talked to him alone, brother-to-brother. When Maha located Cudgo, the outlaw told the posseman he didn't have no brothers, threw out his Schofield and shot Maha through the heart. He stood and emptied the pistol into the Seminole scout, picked up the Henry leaning against his saddle and emptied that into Maha, too; all told, twenty-five .44 bullets.

Maha and Nelson became numbers six and seven on Cudgo's list of murders. The first three were men he wanted to rob. One was a banker walking home from work one evening in Anadarko, second was a mail rider down around old Fort Washita, the third a man out plowing his field. The other two were Indian Lighthorsemen, brother Seminoles on his trail like Maha, who Cudgo had ambushed and left dying. Cudgo had been wanted by the law, Indian and white, going on fourteen years, but had never once been arrested. He'd started out running whiskey to Indians in the Territory, gravitated to armed robbery, usually with assault, and eventually the murder of his victims. Cudgo had always liked to rob, but it got to where he believed he enjoyed the killin' more, especially the lawmen.

Right after assassinating Nelson, the killer rode out of Waurika taking the deputy's horse with him. Went back to his campfire by Honey Creek where he laid down to get a good night's sleep, confident that no one else would come looking for him that night; no one in Waurika, leastwise. The bullet-riddled body of Barna Maha still lay thirty feet from where Cudgo put out his bedroll by the fire, but the outlaw didn't think the posseman would disturb his sleep, neither.

The next morning, leaving Maha's body for the buzzards and coyotes, Cudgo rode northwest. He figured he could trade the horses and guns to some Kiowa or Comanche. Might be able to get something for the rest of their outfits, too; maybe one of them Comanche women for a night or two.

Bass didn't like the news. He'd known Maha and Nelson pretty well, had worked with them both. Barna was a quiet, peaceful man, a Christian; always looking for a man's good side. Nelson was a hard-working and diligent young lawman who left a wife and baby boy. Bass wondered what would happen if his own sons had to grow up without a daddy.

"Gimme that warrant for Cudgo," he said to the court commissioner. "Time that bastard was brung in."

The other deputies hung back. Not that they didn't all want to get Pike Cudgo, especially now that he'd killed some of their own, but they deferred to their big associate. It was unspoken, but all seemed to agree. Maybe because Bass had been around longer than most of them; maybe, like the wanted, it was because he was black and Indian too, even though Cudgo was blooded Seminole, Bass adopted Creek. They all recognized that Bass, amongst all of them, most likely would survive the encounter. Might've been a little fear in some about coming face-to-face with the vicious killer—nothing any of them would admit—but the stark reality was Bass was well-equipped and the most skilled, physically and mentally, to deal with Cudgo. It went without saying, he was the best among them.

Still, Cudgo was exceptionally dangerous and merciless. No man should have to go alone west of the Dead Line—the most perilous country in the Territory—to bring him in, even Bass Reeves. Heck Thomas moved to where the big deputy stood folding the papers, putting them into his warrant book. "I'll go with you, Bass," he said.

Reeves looked up at the young deputy, smiling a bit. He nodded once. "Believe I'd welcome your help, Heck. I'd like to leave out this evenin' if that suits you."

Bass didn't put together the usual outfit. Decided not to take the prisoner wagon, but did hire on a posseman, one he could trust and one who could read, Jud Coldstone. No need for the chow wagon and cook, either. Bass figured they could hire most meals along the way, scare up a rabbit or two. They needed to move swift and as quietly as possible when they got near their quarry. They carried no other writs or warrants. This was a singular mission–to bring in Pike Cudgo, dead or alive. Bass hoped it'd be the latter. They'd likely be a week or more out from Fort Smith when they caught up with the killer; hauling a dead man more than two days wasn't a pleasant thing to do, especially during these warmer months.

"How you figger we's gonna find this Cudgo feller, Bass?" the posseman asked. It was mid-morning of the second day. They'd ridden twenty miles west of Ada where they'd stayed the night with a preacher friend of Bass's, an ally of the law. Not yet nine and the day had already started to burn, promised to be another scorcher.

Bass removed his hat, and wiped the sweat from his brow with his sleeve. He squinted at the sun. "They's a Indin I know figure'll tell us where he's at," he answered.

Deputy Thomas shifted in his saddle, spat tobacco juice to his left, downwind. "What Indin?"

Bass furrowed his brow and reined his roan some to the left, hoping to get a little further out of range of Heck's next spit. "It's said Cudgo likes to stay in amongst the Kiowa and Comanche, 'cause they don't bother him none. He brings 'em whiskey. Ain't no white man much likes to go into that land if they can help it, 'cept them cattle drovers, but they got contracts with the Indins to cross it.

"Old Kiowa chief named Plenty Buffalo likes to keep close tabs on who's comin' in and out of his territory. Likely he'll know where Cudgo is."

"Others ain't been able to track him down, and live to tell about it," Heck said. "Man's been on the scout a long time, Bass. Even old Bud Ledbetter went after him with no luck. How come he didn't consult with that Kiowa you's talking about?"

"Doubt Bud even knowed about that," Bass answered. "Even if he did, that old chief probably wouldn't tell him nothin'. Plenty Buffalo don't much cotton to lawmen or soldiers, even the Indin ones."

"Wull, what makes you so dang special?" asked the posseman.

Bass laughed. "I ain't special, Jud. Don't be thinkin' that. Hell, Plenty Buffalo'd just as soon slit my throat as yours. But the thing is he owes me. I saved his life onest. As much as he'd like to hang my scalp on his lodge pole, he's honor bound not to. So we get along better'n most."

Half the sun had set when the trio rode up to Plenty Bufflalo's village. Dogs announced their approach, an animated chatter began to rise from the curious women and children watching the men ride in. A wizened old man emerged from a tent at the center of the village, and several younger men began to gather at his side. He sat on an old buffalo blanket, looked up at the three visitors, and waited.

The riders stopped twenty yards from the chief and his entourage. "You boys stay on your horses. I'll go talk to him," Bass said in a low voice. He dismounted and walked over to the group, stood waiting for an invitation. The old man motioned with his arm for Reeves to sit, and he did, cross-legged.

"I have not seen you for many long times, Bazreefs," the old man said. He spoke in his own tongue, almost yelling. "Why have you come to my village? Why have you come into my country."

Bass understood most of the Kiowa spoken, but he answered in American. "We seek a man wanted by our laws. These two men with me are lawmen, too. We believe this man is in your land, we hope you know where he is and will tell us." He knew Plenty Buffalo understood him. It was a power game.

The old chief looked long and steely at Reeves before he spoke again, this time in American. "Who is this man you seek?"

"Pike Cudgo," Bass answered.

The Kiowa nodded and grunted. Again, he waited several moments before responding, pondering. "Yes, I know this man. What has he done?"

"Plenty Buffalo knows Cudgo has been selling him whiskey for many years. That is one thing against the law, but the worst is he has killed white and Indian lawmen, like myself."

Plenty Buffalo didn't wait long to reply. "I have no fight against these things. I have killed white men and Indins, too."

"Yes, but that was many years ago when you were at war. The white man's law has forgiven you for that," Bass said.

Plenty Buffalo grunted again. "I think no. We once rode all these plains with many horses, but now the whites bunch us together like the cattle they move, shot our horses, force us to live in this small nation."

Bass thought the discussion was getting away from the purpose at hand. He had no desire to discuss politics with the Kiowa chief. "Plenty Buffalo, is a wise chief," he said. "What he says is truth. But my leaders say we must bring this man in to pay for the killings he's done. He has broken our laws; we must hang him. But that is not all. Anyone who helps him hide, who keeps him from us, will be punished, too. Put in the white man's jail."

The chief's look was even. "I can tell you where he is, or I can tell you I don't know. There is not a way you can know truth in that. If you give something to Plenty Buffalo, to his people, maybe he remembers where this man is."

"What do you want?"

"In this land crowded with Indin peoples, game is scarce. My people go hungry. White men move many long-horned beasts across this land given to Kiowa and our Comanche brothers. We want more of those to eat."

"The cattlemen already pay you for that," Bass replied. "They give you beef to eat."

"Ungh, this is so," said Plenty Buffalo. "But we need more. For words to give you of this man you seek, I have need . . . five long-horns."

Bass sighed and nodded. "Is that it?"

Plenty Buffalo thought for a moment. "If I tell you where this Cudgo is, I will get no more whiskey. You give me two bottle."

"I can get you these long-horns, but it will take a few days," Bass said. He shook his head. "I cannot give you whiskey. Plenty Buffalo knows that is against my laws."

The chief looked at the sky and muttered something in Kiowa. "What about horse?" he asked. "We have few horses. Your law against giving me horse?"

"I will give you the long-horns first." The deputy stood. "After I capture Cudgo, I will give you his horse."

Plenty Buffalo thought about it a while, then he consulted with two of his men. He turned back to Bass. "Look to north," he said at last. "Walking Crow say he met him one moon past near the long knife fort."

"Fort Sill?"

The Indian nodded. “Told him would not have whiskey for a while. Going to follow creek into the rock mountains.”

Pike Cudgo retreated up into a rugged range of old mountains thrust up half a billion years ago. Over the eons some of the once majestic peaks of the Wichitas, weathered by wind and rain, ice and oceans, had worn down to twenty-five hundred foot high knobs and crests of rounded granite boulders and craggy mesas. High banked and narrow creeks cut through tumbles of cliffs and bluffs winding deep and swift as they fell to the low lands. Hardy vegetation grew on the sides of hills where ages of erosion gave them a meager soil in which they could survive. Forests of tenacious red cedars, dense clusters of post oak and blackjack crowded among the scattered sarsens and cairns old glaciers had long since carved, crumbled and left in stacked pieces. In the high meadows tough prairie grasses of bluestem, switchgrass and side oats sprung up strong enough to endure the fierce cold of the winters and drought-heat of the summers. Here, a singular hackberry stood sentinel over a meadow, a refuge from the heat and cold for the resilient foraging wild things; there, a group of the trees huddled in reserve.

Not many humans came to this rough country, even the Comanche and Kiowa and Cheyenne to whom the U.S. government had given the land. Elk and deer and other game roamed fairly plentiful, but these were horse-culture people preferring to race across the plains in a hunt for the buffalo. This synergy didn’t fit well in these fractured, rocky

Wichitas. Still, the Indians came to hunt when a lack of game on the prairie pressed them to do so.

Rumors in the white world said gold might be found in these mountains, and a few had come looking. Turned out to be a bust, though; the prospectors left as quickly as they'd come. Some returned to civilization, some just vanished. A few stayed long enough to put up shacks while they dug in the rocks. Those huts still standing had long since been abandoned, too. Cudgo holed-up in one of these. Figured his killing federal officers would make the hunt for him more immediate, more intense. He also figured he could stay well concealed back in the Wichitas, protected by the terrain and his Indian customers who did not want to lose him as their supplier of whiskey.

"Yonder, Bass," Heck said, pointing to a ridge across the half-mile stretch of meadow.

"See 'em," Reeves replied. The trio of lawmen kept their horses at a walk.

"Looks to be four of 'em," Jud said. "Could be more back t'other side the ridge."

"Comanche, you figure, or Kiowa?" Heck asked.

"Cheyenne," Bass said. "Think I recognize one of the horses. That big red paint in the middle; believe his rider is a man called Yells at a Bear."

Deputy Thomas looked askance at Deputy Reeves, shaking his head with an incredulous laugh. "You know all these Indins out here?"

Bass kept his eye on the party of horsemen at the ridge. "Jist the important ones. Most likely they's out here huntin'.

Let's go parlay with 'em." He gave his roan a gentle kick starting him forward at a trot.

The party of hunters waited as the three approached them. The closer they got, Deputy Reeves became more convinced the Cheyenne Yells at a Bear sat astride the paint horse. That was a stroke of luck, as Bass spoke little Cheyenne, but knew the Indian leader of the group spoke passable American.

The lawmen stopped twenty yards from the Indians. They sat sizing each other up for a while before Bass spoke. "You are Yells at a Bear, a great leader of the Cheyenne people." Reeves paused, letting his compliment and the vanity of being recognized settle in with the man. He watched the Indian sit higher, throwing his shoulders back slightly in a show of pride. He nodded once, keeping his stern look back at the black lawman. Bass waited.

"You black white lawman the peoples call Shoots with Both Eyes. You eated my camp, many . . . long go."

"Yes, Rides Two Horses and his people fed me good, gave me warm buffalo robes for sleeping. How is the elder?"

"His dead. Fever make dead."

"Umph." Bass nodded. "Too bad. A great elder."

"Umph," Yells at a Bear responded with his own nod.

Bass got to the point. "We have come to find a man. He has broken our laws, killed lawmen. We think he is here in the stone mountains. We must take him with us. He is called Cudgo."

Yells at a Bear remained quiet for a few moments before turning to his brothers to confer in Cheyenne. Turning back to Reeves he said, "Know this man. Not like. His not good man. Sell whiskey the peoples, make all crazy. Not good.

"I take you. You take Cudgo, give me his horse."

Bass furrowed his brow, shook his head. "I cannot. I have already promised his horse to the Kiowa, Plenty Buffalo. But if you help us capture him, you can come to the fort and I will get you two horses."

Yells at a Bear nodded at the offer, turned to the others and explained the deal. A short argument followed. Looking back at Bass, the Indian said, "Three horse."

Bass sighed. "Three horses," he acknowledged.

The Cheyenne group led the lawmen down a steep slope, moving single-file on a narrow switchback. The nimble ponies of the Indians had taken them some fifty yards out ahead of the lawmen.

"Three horses to these Cheyenne; five beeves to the Kiowa," Heck re-counted from his saddle five yards behind Reeves. "How is it you're gonna manage all this tradin', Bass?" he asked.

"Ain't quite figgered that part out yet," Bass responded.

"Now, ain't that a fine kettle uh corn," Jud interjected from the rear. "You're gonna end up getting' our hides skint, Bass."

"Ain't I always brung you back safe, Jud?"

Coldstone let out a hoot. "Wull, you did allus brung me back. I ain't so sure 'bout the safe part. I recall that time with Dick Glass."

Bass didn't comment. The incident had happened before his deputying days when the freedman outlaw Glass had come upon their camp, beaten him severely and shot Jud, leaving them both for dead after taking the moonshine they'd just made. "We're jist gonna have to find us a trail herd, and do some negotiatin' with the ramrod," Reeves said. "Believe I can get the court to pick that up. And when we get back at Fort Sill I 'spect that colonel be happy to part with three horses if it mean gettin' Pike Cudgo gone, and keepin' them Indins sober."

"Sure hope all that don't cut into our fees from the court," Heck said.

"If it do, I make it up to you from my own pocket, Heck. 'Portant thing is gettin' Cudgo out t'way of killin' anybody else, be he in jail or dead."

Bass didn't look back at Deputy Thomas. The silence from his young colleague, as they rode along, had the sound of contrition.

They'd come to the bottom of a narrow cut, a shallow creek running through it. The Cheyenne waited for the lawmen to catch up, their mounts standing ankle-deep in the swift water, drinking. When Bass's roan reached the bottom of the cut, Yells at a Bear turned and started upstream, his men following. They moved up the creek for twenty minutes before the Indians went to the left bank climbing the slope which rose much less severe than the one they'd come down a mile back.

At the crest they turned right, followed the gently rising ridge toward a grassy saddle between two flint-capped hills. Beyond the cul, a meadow dipped for a quarter mile then rose into the distance ending at the base of a craggy granite mesa. Yells at a Bear and his group stopped.

Bass walked his roan up next to the Cheyenne leader's paint, waited for the rider to speak. The warrior pointed.

"At bottom of flat rock hill, back in short gulch is old hut. Pie-Cuggo stay here. Cliff at back. Front only out."

Bass squinted at the mesa, pondering. He pulled makings from his shirt pocket and started building a smoke, glancing up at the mesa every now and then. Stuck the rolled smoke into one corner of his mouth, and put away the makings. Dug a wooden match from a front vest pocket, struck it into flame with a thumb nail, held the cupped fire to the end of the smoke. He removed the cigarette, pursed his lips and blew out the match.

"Whadda you figure, half day's ride?" he asked the Cheyenne.

"Maybe," Yells at a Bear answered. He pointed again.

Bass studied the sky above the mesa, the horizon at either side of it. A high dark blue-gray mass spread across half the heavens. "Yeah, I seen that," he said.

Deputy Thomas rode up beside the two. "Looks to be a storm brewin'," he said.

"Looks t'be," Bass responded.

Late afternoon had come when they reached the mouth of the mesa canyon. A good four hours of daylight still remained, but the skies of the gathering storm promised to hamper that some. Ragged blue-black advance clouds swirled below the bubbled underbelly of the thunderhead, and a rumble behind the mesa forewarned the storm's approach. The wind in the darkening started to swirl through the canyon rushing out and up and back as if confused at its aim, yet anxious to its purpose. Dust, small bits of canyon debris blew into the men, forcing them to lower their heads and squint.

The shack they hoped still held Cudgo sat four hundred yards up the winding arroyo. The warrior Yells at a Bear sent to scout the hut, reported an unsaddled horse grazed nearby it, that the hut's chimney had a curl of smoke curled.

Bass looked up the walls of the canyon, then at the swarming sky. He eyed the Cheyenne leader and shouted into the wind, "I wanted to send some of your men up along the canyon rim, so they'd have the high ground around the shack, but don't think we can do that now." He looked up, mashing his hand atop of his hat to hold it there. "Looks like this storm gonna mean use some caution." A bolt of lightning cracked up on the rim, followed in seconds by another further up, making his point. "They'd be sittin' ducks for this lightnin'," he added.

Yells at a Bear nodded. He made a snake-like motion with his hand and arm, yelled through the howl at the lawman, "We go along canyon wall. Can hide in rock near side of hut. You go other side. Plenty rock for safe. Storm keep Cuggo inside. Not hear us outside."

"Reckon that'll have to work," Bass said. He turned to Deputy Thomas and the posseman who hunkered behind him.

"Heck, you and Jud and me'll try to spread out some when we get near the shack. Yells at a Bear's man said it don't look like Cudgo can 'scape out t'back, but jist the same, we needs to make sure."

The two groups moved up the canyon trying to stay hidden, the funneled wind and grit whistling through the chasm aided their stealth. A group of boulders along the left side gave the Cheyenne concealment about thirty yards from the cabin. The lawmen trio had less cover, but managed to crouch behind a waist high cluster of rocks next to a bushy old red cedar swaying wildly. Forty yards away sat the shack.

Bass spoke to the posseman. “Jud, work your way to the back corner of the cabin. Don’t know if he can get out t’back, but in case he do, you cover it.

He turned to the other deputy. “Heck, you stay here. Cover me and the front, that side windah, too. I’m gonna go up to the front, see if I can’t call him out.”

“You think that’s a good idea, Bass?” Thomas asked. “Seems to me you’d be awful exposed getting’ up there.”

A sudden lightning flash and crash resounded directly overhead. Fat drops of rain started to hit the dusty ground, its intensity increasing with each second, swirling in the wind.

Bass looked up into the rain. “Believe this rain’ll make me a tougher target. Ain’t sure he could hear me from here. Ain’t sure he knows we’s out here, neither. ’Sides, Cudgo may not be the one in there. Ain’t nobody’s seen him yet.”

Jud moved at a running crouch to the front corner of the cabin, progressed along the wall, and under the sill of the shuttered window. By the time he got to the back corner, the rain started coming in sheets.

Bass broke at a run for the front of the shack. Charged against the wind, sloshing through sudden puddles and new mud. The storm at its full fury, boomed and hissed , strobing the near-darkness with its constant discharges. At about his halfway point, a rifle shot rang out from the front window, barely distinguishable in the tempest din inside the echoing canyon walls. Splinters of bark flew above Heck’s head where a .44 slug hit the cedar tree.

Seeing the muzzle flash, Bass dodged and rolled across his shoulders and back, came to his feet again, recovered his hat, sprinted the final ten yards to the front corner of the shack. The shot missed him, but he expected more. If not Cudgo in the shack, was damn sure someone hostile.

Bass drew out his Colt, muddied at the butt from his roll. He grasped the cylinder and held the handle out to the rain, letting the downpour wash it off, hoping it would still fire.

"Pike Cudgo? That you in there?" he hollered. No answer came from the cabin.

"I reckon if you wasn't Pike Cudgo, you'd uh said so," he yelled again, waiting another ten seconds. "This here is Federal Deputy Marshal Bass Reeves!" Still no answer.

"I have a warrant to arrest you for the murder of Deputy U.S. Marshal B.P. Nelson and his posseman, Barna Maha, a citizen of the Seminole Nation!"

Rain battered the shack, the ground and rocks, wind tore through the canyon, lightning and thunder flashed, boomed like cannon fire. No sound came from inside.

Bass continued. "You need to lay down your arms and come on out. I got a passel of men out here and we got you surrounded. We aim to take you back to Fort Smith dead or alive. Be in your best interest if'n you's to decide to make it alive."

"I know who you are," came a voice from the cabin. "You can take that paper on me and shove it up yer ass, 'cause you damn sure ain't servin' it on me; you or no other goddam sumbitch of a marshal."

The rain had started to abate some. Bass looked up at the sky. "You'd jist as soon come on out, Cudgo. Soon as this storm passes we'll smoke you out. Got some Cheyenne out here itchin' to do some such as that. You ain't getting' away. Why can't you jist give up?"

"'Cause I ain't ridin' back to Fort Smith chained up in no goddam prisoner wagon, just to face a hangin'."

Cudgo raised his voice so the others could hear him. "'Sides, them Cheyenne boys is on *my* side. They like the whiskey I sells 'em. Don't ya, boys? Don't reckon you'd want to give that up, now would ya?"

Reeves answered for the Cheyenne. "Not these, Cudgo. This here's Yells at a Bear and his band. Don't think he much cares for you."

Quiet came from the cabin for a few moments, then in barely more than a mumble, "That sumbitch injun has allus been a prick," Cudgo said.

The rain had become a patter, the bulk of the storm moving on to the southeast, the day inside the vertical walls of the canyon started to become noticeably brighter with myriad falls cascading from the rock rim. The sun had gone down far enough so that its direct rays no longer reached the canyon floor.

Another rifle shot came from a crack in the window cover, and the head of one of the Cheyenne snapped backwards. The warrior tumbled, splashing dead into the red mud behind him. One of his brothers let out a war cry, stood and fired back at the window twice in rapid succession. Some of the rough cedar boards covering the opening shattered a foot from Bass's right elbow.

Cudgo returned the fire almost immediately and the second warrior spun to the ground with a bullet wound to his upper right chest.

Reeves motioned angrily toward the Cheyenne position. "Hold on! Hold on!" he shouted.

"Damnation, Cudgo! You sure ain't makin' it any easier on yourself. Whatever whiskey sellin' good will you had with them Cheyenne is ruint now. Oncest we get you outta there, it's gonna take all I can to keep Yells at a Bear from skinnin' you alive."

"Not if I shoot his sumbitch injun ass first," came Cudgo's response. Another shot exploded from the window, whanging off a boulder at the Cheyenne position.

Reeves slammed the barrel of his pistol twice against the window covering. "I'm givin' you fifteen seconds to come on out with your hands up, Cudgo. If you don't, we're gonna open up on ya. We ain't gonna let this go past dark. Don't figure this shack can hold back too many rounds of rifle fire."

Bass broke for a small clump of boulders near the canyon wall, out of the line of sight of the cabin front window from which Cudgo had fired. Once at the rocks, he moved quickly at a crouch to Deputy Thomas's position. Cudgo spotted him, and sent off another shot, hitting the canyon wall behind Reeves.

The rain had almost stopped. "Ten seconds, Cudgo!" Bass hollered. He motioned for Jud to move away from the cabin, which he did trying to hide behind a small cedar near the base of the wall.

"Last chance to come out alive, Cudgo!" Reeves yelled. He waited another few seconds.

"Aw right, then. Let's shoot him out of there, boys." Reeves fired his pistol; the others followed in a thunderous volley lasting thirty seconds. The thin wood of the shack exploded with every impact. They all stopped to reload, waiting for return fire, but none came.

Reeves looked cautiously around the trunk of the cedar. “Had enough, Cudgo?” he asked. He got no response.

“Think we got him, Bass,” Deputy Thomas said.

“Cain’t be too sure,” Reeves said. “He might be waitin’ for us all to walk up there so’s we’d be easier targets.” He looked around at the canyon, then at the patch of indigo sky above the rim. Most of the clouds had cleared, and two bright stars had come out. “Getting’ dark quick,” he added. Deep shadows started to fill the canyon.

A rifle shot echoed from the posseman’s position, followed by a loud holler and curse, then another rifle shot. “Jud?” Reeves yelled, but got no response.

Bass started moving through the shadows toward Jud’s location, Heck followed. They found Jud sprawled behind a boulder, a splotch of blood spread across his rain-soaked shirt at the abdomen. Both the deputies crouched, looking about furtively.

Coldstone groaned, grabbing at the wound on his left side. Reeves grabbed the posseman’s shoulder. “Jud,” he said in a whisper, letting the man know it was him. “What happened?”

“He come up on me out t’dark, like one of them Cheyenne,” Coldstone said with a grimace. “Surprised me. Didn’t expect anyone coulda survived inside that shack with the shootin’ we done. Never seen him come out, never seen him ’til it was almost too late. Ain’t no back door to that place. I looked.” He looked down at his side, raising his bloodied hand off the wound. “Damn,” he added.

“Musta come out through the roof,” Bass said.

"He's comin' at me with a knife, and I swung down on him with my barrel, whacked him good on the shoulder. Rifle fired when I done that, but it went wide. He's aimin' that knife for my heart, but stabbed me here in the side when I whacked him. I brung up my boot, kickin' him backards, got off another shot. Believe I got him that time 'bout the same spot he got me with that knife. Then he run off. Had that knife, but didn't look like he's carryin' no other arms."

Bass stood and yelled into the gathering darkness, "Cudgo's out here! Look sharp!" Hoping Yells at a Bear and his boys would understand him.

They heard the sounds of a scuffle over near where the Indians had holed up, then a rifle shot followed by confused loud voices speaking Cheyenne.

"Heck, you stay with Jud," Bass said and took off at a run. He knew if Cudgo got past the Indians, and out of the canyon to their horses, he'd never be able to chase him in the dark, not in the Wichitas. That ground proved hard to traverse even in broad daylight.

He moved through the canyon cautiously, not wanting an ambush. Didn't figure Cudgo would slow down long enough to jump him. Still . . .

Yells at a Bear and what was left of the band of Cheyenne, followed the deputy. When they reached the mouth of the canyon, they found one of the Indian ponies gone; not unexpected, but surprising that Cudgo didn't take one of the saddled horses. Maybe in his haste and wounded state, he took the first horse he came to; maybe he knew the pony was better suited for the treacherous terrain.

Yells at a Bear squatted near the horses, studying the tracks, and the ground around them. A gibbous moon hung in the dusky sky, light enough for the sharp-eyed Indian to pick up sign.

"Blood on rock, ground. His got wound."

"Jud said he shot him," Bass said.

The Cheyenne leader stood. "His shoot another Cheyenne, take rifle." He motioned with his arm and hand across the sloping meadow to the southeast. "Ride toward fort, storm."

"See to your wounded," Bass said to Yells at a Bear. Went to his horse and mounted up. "Gonna try to chase him down. Figure that wound'll slow him some. Might even stop him 'fore I do."

"Watch close," the Cheyenne cautioned. "Hunts bear with wound more danger."

Bass nodded. " 'Preciate the thought."

The night hampered finding sign, but the moonlight did help some. What he could read told him what he'd figured: Cudgo had turned more south. Bass suspected the man wanted to get to some Kiowa or Comanche village, some place they'd take him in and protect him. Cudgo wasn't exactly well-liked among the Indians, but they tolerated him for what he provided. His trade made him some allies among the tribes, more so than the men of the whites' law. His black skin didn't give him an in, though. Many of the Kiowa and Comanche remembered Adobe Walls and Palo Duro, the Buffalo Soldiers. Reds and blacks had many bitter battles between them. Cudgo and the plains Indian had, at best, an uneasy alliance.

The moon set before daylight came, the unsure ground in the dark forced Bass to stop and dismount. Last thing he needed was his big roan to stumble and break a leg among these sharp rocks; or worse, throw him into them. Less than two hours until daylight; he would wait.

The previous evening's storm had filled the rocky rills in the high meadow, and Bass heard the trickle of running water nearby. He followed the sound in the near dark, squatting to scoop the cold water in his hand to drink. His stomach reminded him he hadn't eaten in a while, thought a couple corn dodgers remained in his bags. Back at the roan, digging in the saddlebag, he looked east. Above the black of the jagged skyline, he saw a sliver of pink, but a maelstrom of stars still glittered the firmament. Meadow birds had not yet started to stir; not a sound of anything disturbed the pre-dawn except the breathing of his horse. The morning was clear and still and crisp.

Something twitched in the dark, itching the back of his sixth sense, and made him turn around. Out in the dimness, ever so faintly in the starlight, he saw a glint, and his instinct threw him to the ground. Saw a muzzle flash some thirty yards away, and just before he hit the ground a rifle shot cracked.

The roan screamed and bolted. Bass lay flat and drew out his Colt, started crawling to a dark clump of rocks five yards to his right front. A second shot boomed, and the ground erupted inches from his left leg. Felt the big slug burrow through the dirt below his kneecap. He reached the rocks, and drew his body and legs behind them, peeking around the cover, looking out where he thought he'd seen the gunfire. Saw no movement.

"Cudgo?" Bass waited for an answer, but none came.

"I know you're shot, Cudgo. You give it up, we'll take care of ya. Get you back to Fort Sill, have that Army doctor fix ya up. Wasn't you once with the Tenth Cavalry? They'll take care of an old soldier."

"Ain't aimin' to do that, Marshal." Reeves could hear pain in the voice and the tiredness. He figured the outlaw had lost a lot of blood.

"No need to do this, Cudgo. I can wait you out. Believe you'll bleed to death in an hour or so, mebbe less. You keep shootin' at me, I'll shoot back. Pretty sure I can hit you, oncest I sees where you's at. Ain't no need to die like this."

"You want me to live so you can take me back to Fort Smith to hang? Naw, Reeves. Only reason I'm here now is my horse fell and broke his neck. Naw, I'm gonna kill you, gonna take your horse and ride on outta here. Don't need no goddam cuttin' on by a white army doctor. Know a Comanche woman that'll take care of me better."

Reeves figured he'd better move. Conversation with Cudgo probably helped the outlaw pin down his location. The morning had become a little grayer. Concealment would start to become harder by the minute. He looked about and spotted another, bigger group of boulders out to his right front, and started crawling through the bluestem toward them.

When he rounded the back side of the boulders, a faint shadow stopped him, and he looked up, right into the rifle bore of a Henry .45.

"Figured you'd head for these rocks," Pike Cudgo said. He weaved slightly where he stood, cocked the hammer back on the Henry taking aim at Bass's forehead. The deputy watched the outlaw's right forefinger start to tighten on the trigger.

Another shadow appeared swiftly behind Cudgo and delivered a smashing blow to the back of the outlaw's head with a pistol barrel. Bass had reflexively curled his head and shoulders away from the end of the rifle which discharged a fraction of a second later. The bullet from the Henry cratered the ground a few inches behind Bass's head, and the unconscious outlaw fell, like a two hundred and twenty pound sack of potatoes, on top of the deputy.

Someone rolled Cudgo off Bass.

"You okay, Bass?" Deputy Thomas asked.

Reeves looked up. "When did you get here?"

"Mebbe thirty minutes ago. When that Cheyenne told me what you's doin', I followed ya. Been hidin' in the grass over yonder." He motioned with his head.

"Well, Damn, Heck. Why didn't you just shoot the bastard? He come close to blowin' my brains out."

"I's too close. 'Fraid it'd uh gone through him and hit you, so I just run up and coldcocked him."

Bass propped himself on an elbow and looked at the laid out outlaw. "Reckon you killed him?"

"Ain't sure," Heck said. He felt Cudgo's neck with a finger, pushed an eyelid open.

"Nah, it don't look like it. Reckon he'll have a dang good headache, though."

"How's Jud?"

"He'll be awright, but we ought to get him some doctorin' pretty soon. Tough old bastard."

Bass smiled. "He is that," he said. "What about the Cheyenne?"

“One of ’em dead, two of ’em wounded. One’ll probably make it, ain’t so sure ’bout t’other.” He leaned against a boulder and looked over at the out-cold killer. “That Pike Cudgo is one mean sumbitch.”

Bass got to his feet. “Well, let’s get this mean sumbitch put up in irons, and haul him off to Fort Sill afore he bleeds to death. Oncest he gets strong enough to travel, we’ll commence bringing him in to Judge Parker.

# Freed Men

From an interview with Jud Coldstone of the Creek Nation—posseman, guard, and cook to lawmen of the U.S. Court for the Western District of Arkansas, most often for Deputy U.S. Marshal Bass Reeves:

*Bass growed up a slave, borned around 1840. He weren't for sure on the exact date, and the records ain't clear on that, neither. So he took the 4th of July. Cain't say who his daddy was, but his momma's name was Pearlalee. She brought him into the world over in western Arkansas, Crawford County; he's owned by a politician named William Reeves who cropped some land there. Like most slaves, Bass took his master's last name.*

*Said when he's old enough to do the work, musta been about age five, he was a field hand, a water boy. Later he was put on as the black smith's helper. It was during this time they discovered he had a way with the mules and horses, so he was put to tendin' the master's prize steeds, and the animals thrived.*

*The boy grew, too. Workin' in that smithy's barn he become a strappin' young man. By eighteen he stood well over six foot, and had shoulders broad as an ax handle is long. Most likely because of his size and strength, Mister William Reeves selected Bass as his personal servant and bodyguard; become the man's constant companion.*

*At one point Bass asked Marse William, as he referred to him, if'n he'd teach him to read and write, but of course his master refused. It were pretty much an unwritten law back in them days that no slave was to ever be allowed readin' and writin'. He did teach him how to handle firearms and shoot, though. That become a smart move, because it turned out Bass had keen eyes and steady hands. He become a dead shot usin' either, which pleased his master, who could not shoot worth beans. But he was a bettin' man and he entered Bass in all the turkey shoots around, which he never failed to win. Bass got a reputation makin' it more harder for him to get in the competitions, so old Mister William would say, "Tell you what, I'll have m'boy shoot left-handed so's to make it more evener agin you fellas." Most agreed to that, 'course, none of 'em knowed that Bass could shoot a vee jist as good with his left eye as he could his right.*

*Bass said when he's a boy of about eight, old William packed up his whole bunch in Arkansas—children, in-laws, livestock and slaves—some thirty wagons, and hauled 'em all off down to Grayson County in the new state of Texas. When the States War started, William's boy George joined up with the Eleventh Texas Cavalry formed there in Grayson County, takin' the rank of captain. Ended up a colonel before it were all said and done. Cap'n George took Bass along as his personal servant, and it was during that time Bass parted company with Reeves and his slavery in a none too harmonious way.*

The sudden encounter froze the young slave in his tracks.

A creek ran not far from where his colonel's Texas outfit stopped to bivouac, and Bass had gone down there to fetch water. It was colder than a snake's belly, but Marse Reeves had in mind to wash up some, so he'd sent Bass out there to get a couple buckets.

That's when he'd come face-to-face with the Yankee. Least he thought he was a Yankee, as the man had a Union Army Colt pointed at his nose.

Around Colonel Reeve's tent, Bass heard things. Knew they was in Arkansas, up north from Fort Smith. The officers talked about a place called Leetown where they was said to be a bunch of Unionists, and north of that, the place General McCulloch's boys had set up camp. Called it Twelve Corner Church.

He'd gone down a slope toward the creek about two hundred yards from the camp, and had just rounded a big mossy boulder at the creek's edge when he found himself looking down the bore of that pistol.

The dreadful click of the cocked-back hammer, fixed him. He dropped the buckets and raised his hands high above his head.

"What you doin' out here, boy?" The man asked in a whisper.

"Fetchin' water, suh," Bass responded.

The Yankee stayed crouched behind the rock, raising his head a little to peer over it, looking up into the woods. "Anyone else with ya?" he asked.

"No suh, jus' me," Bass answered.

He only suspected the man was a Yankee, because of that Colt pointed at him, but not much else told him so. Didn't wear no Yankee uniform, looked more like a cowboy or one of them buffalo skinners. Had long sandy-colored hair down to his shoulders and a thick hanging mustache below a big sloping nose. Wore a broad-brimmed leather hat and a long canvas coat. He and all his clothes looked plenty trail-worn.

"You a Yankee?" Bass asked.

The man stood, still looking about, but keeping his pistol pointed at Bass. He ignored the question.

"Turn around," the man said. "Put your hands behind your back."

"You takin' me prisoner?" Bass asked.

"Shut up. You yell out, or anything stupid like that, and I'll blow your brains out."

Bass obeyed, keeping his mouth shut. The man tied the slave's hands behind his back.

"C'mon." He yanked Bass by the back of his arm, and pushed him along in front. They headed into the woods, away from where the Texans camped. Crossed the creek and went up the slope; after about a thirty minute tramp, the man pulled Bass to a stop.

"Sit down," he told Bass, pushing him against a tree. Bass sat cross-legged at the base of the oak and his captor crouched five feet away, opened his long coat and pulled out a shoulder gun stock which he mounted onto the butt of his revolver.

The man put the gun to his shoulder and sighted down the barrel, pointing it out through the trees. Then he sat, too, leaning back against a sycamore. They stayed that way for some time, neither speaking, waiting. Darkness started coming on.

"Bet you're a slave." The statement made Bass jump, the sound of it startling in the cold forest silence. He nodded.

"You belong to that Texas colonel, don't ya; one rides the big black."

"How you know that?" Bass asked.

"Hell, son, it's my job to know," the man answered.

"So you *is* a Yankee. You's a Yankee spy," Bass said.

The man grinned, not acknowledging his prisoner's indictment. Looking about, Bass could see the light of small fires dotting the dark forest around them. The man stood and leaned his piece against the tree trunk.

"Believe we could use a fire, too," he said. "Gonna be a long cold night."

"Thems all Union fires you see," he added. "And if I know my Rebs, ain't none of 'em going to come out looking for us tonight. They'll save that for first light."

The warmth of the small blaze kept the chill away from Bass's front side, but his back and legs grew numb from sitting. His bound hands ached with cold.

"Mistuh, I gots to piss," he said.

The Yankee looked at him through dark eyes. "Awright, but I'll damn well shoot you if you try to get away or fight me," he said.

"Ain't aim to do that. Jus' needs uh piss," Bass said.

"Well, a man's damn sure gotta piss ever now and then." The Yankee helped Bass to his feet, still holding his pistol on him. The young negro stood a head above the white man.

"Turn around," the Yankee said. He untied Bass and let him do his business.

After, Bass leaned against the tree and shook his legs one at a time to get circulation back into them. He squatted in front of the fire and put his hands toward the flames, rubbing them. The Yankee stood five feet away on the other side of the fire, the barrel of his extended Colt resting in the crook of his arm. He made no move to re-bind Bass's hands.

"'Spect you're hungry," the Yankee said. "All's I got is this here jerky." He took two strips of the dried meat from a pocket inside his coat and handed one to Bass. The slave readily accepted it, biting off a chew.

The Yankee watched Bass eat. "What's your name, boy?" he asked.

"My momma name me Bass after her daddy. Las' name Reeves, same as my massuh. All us belongs t'him called Reeves."

The man nodded, still looking at Bass with his coal-black eyes. "You like bein' a slave, Bass?" he asked.

Bass chewed another bite of jerky and put his hands out toward the fire again, thinking about his answer.

"On't know." He shrugged. "Alls I ever know. Marse Reeves, he don't treat me bad. Give me food t'eat, place to sleep. Give me clothes. Ain't nevuh whip me much. He mistress good to my momma and sistuh, too. They works in the big house."

"That all you ever expect to do? Ain't you ever wanted to get free; do things you wanted to do yourself, go wherever you want to go without nobody telling you when and where?"

The Yankee waited for a response, but none came. Bass looked into the fire, chewed the jerky.

After a bit, his captor added, "Wouldn't you like to take a piss without gettin' another man's permission?"

Bass looked up at him, jaw muscles moving; he turned his gaze back to the fire.

The Yankee let it go, changed the subject, shifted his weight on his butt. "'Spect there's gonna be a fight here tomorrow. Mess of Rebs up north. Looks like old Van

Dorn's trying to get 'em around behind us. Them Texas boys of your'n look to be comin' down the road yonder to meet us." He gestured with the gun barrel through the dark trees. "We'll be ready for 'em."

"Where you from, Yank?" Bass asked.

The man stared at Reeves squarely before looking into the fire. "Kansas, mostly," he said. "Rode with General Lane's Jayhawkers. He didn't much cotton to secessionists . . . or slave owners. Called himself an 'abolitionist.'"

"That why you rode with him? You uh . . . ab-bol-lishnest?"

The Yankee threw back his head and laughed. Stood and walked out to the edge of the firelight to take his own piss, chuckling to himself as he did so.

When he came back to the fire, he sat again opposite Reeves, stirred the coals with a stick, threw on another piece of wood.

"You even know what that means, boy? Abolitionist? "

"Sho' I does," Bass answered, a little indignant. "It mean freein' slaves."

"Seems to me the only freed men is the dead ones," his captor said. He paused to stir the fire some more, looked at Bass. "I've personally freed a few myself," he said with a grin and a wink.

"Naw, I rode with Lane because he offered me the job," he continued. "Pay wasn't much, but it kept me out of jail. I needed that more than money at the time.

"Still, sayin' it's legal to own a man don't seem right to me. Sure as hell don't believe I'd put up with anyone claimin' they owned me."

Silence fell between the pair again. The haunting sound of a harmonica drifted in with the cold night air. Men's voices echoed through the black forest; voices in calm conversation and some laughter, distant but clear like coming across a still river at night.

“”Whas yo name, then?” Bass asked. Another long pause followed before the Yankee answered.

“I got several names. Go by Haycock in this here army, William Haycock. Back in Kansas some folks called me ‘Wild Bill.’ Called me that because of the shape of my nose, made fun of how it swoops out sorta like a duck's bill. I didn't much like it at first, made a few callin' me that pay. But now I believe I like it . . . yes sir, believe I do. You can call me Wild Bill.”

Bass nodded, and grinned back at the man. “Wild Bill,” he repeated.

“You realize I'm only telling you this ’cause you'll dead before sundown tomorrow.”

Bass looked cold-eyed at Haycock. “You gone kill me, Wild Bill?” he asked.

Haycock laughed again. “Naw, I ain't gonna kill you, Bass. I'm gonna let you go. But boys see a nigger runnin' free through these here woods, I figure one side or t'other's bound to shoot your ass. Ain't that what we're fightin' for? To set your likes free?” He cocked an eyebrow and grinned at his captive.

Bass stared back at Haycock. After a bit, he said to him, “You frees me, Wild Bill, how you know I ain't finds myself a gun an' free *yo'* ass?”

The Yankee continued to grin back at Bass. After a few seconds Haycock began to sputter through his teeth, then his chest bucked. His eyes squinted as snorts of laughter welled up from his gut and burst out his mouth. His guffaws seemed uncontrollable, mounting. And it started to infect Bass. He grinned; began to laugh, too. As Haycock's hysteria grew, so did Bass's and both men fell back holding their sides, rolling with laughter. The mutual merriment continued a good two minutes, finally subsiding down to snickers.

Haycock sighed out the last remnants of his laughter, wiped his eyes. "Well, Bass, we best get some sleep. I reckon tomorrow's goin' to be a busy day."

The roll of distant thunder popped Bass's eyes open. The world looked gray and cold, trees close by black and wet, fading into fog. His mind swam with confusion. He lay curled up next to what was left of the fire. It came to him suddenly, remembering where he was. More booms sounded. That wasn't no thunder, he realized, it be cannon fire. He sat up quickly and looked about, frightened. His captor was nowhere in sight.

On his feet he heard the clatter of movement behind him, out to his left and down the slope some, toward the road. It sounded like the rustle of many men stirring, a group of soldiers moving. He turned to follow the sound.

Remembering what Haycock had said, he moved quietly, concealed inside the dark cloak of woods and fog. If he could find the road Wild Bill spoke of, follow it north, figured he'd eventually find his colonel's camp. The fog began to lift some, thinning into drifting wisps as daylight increased, and he spied the road some twenty yards to his front. Heading toward it, thought it best to stay in the woods.

The sound of a loping horse approached, and he crouched behind a thicket of blackberry brambles and sumac hoping they, and the fog, stood thick enough to hide him. A lone rider loomed out of the mist, a tall man in the saddle. The horseman wore a wide drooping hat, a dark gray coat and black pants. He had a big Walker Colt strapped to his waist and a Henry repeating rifle in a saddle mounted boot. It wasn't no Confederate uniform he wore, but Bass knew who it was . . . that he was riding his gray mare straight into an ambush.

Just as Bass stood to warn the general, two rifle shots popped almost simultaneously. The balls struck the rider in the chest flipping him backwards off the gray. Bass had seen more than once the devastation a .58 caliber Minie ball could do to human flesh. With two such to the heart, he had little doubt the general died before hitting the ground.

Bass stood frozen in horror, mouth-opened in disbelief. Finally, his sense of vulnerability returned, and he ducked back into the deeper woods for cover, running away from the immediate danger he felt. A human shadow moved out from behind a tree in front of him; Bass slid to a stop, going to his knees. The man cocked a gun held at his shoulder, pointed at Bass's head. He'd looked down the bore of that Army Colt before, now mounted to a shoulder stock.

Haycock raised the barrel of the gun. "Damn, Bass, I just about blowed your head off."

Reeves, still shaken, panting, looked up at Haycock. "They shot McCulloch. I just seen General McCulloch kilt."

"Yeah, that old Ranger hisself," Haycock said, shaking his head. "Just like him to come riding out here to look around instead of sending his scouts. Well, I guess he won't be doing that no more. He's a free man now."

Bass looked up suspiciously at Haycock. "Was you one who shot the general, Wild Bill?" he asked.

Haycock lowered his gun again. "You best get on out of here, Bass, before any of these Missouri boys around here finds ya. Doubt they'd treat you as kindly as I have.

"Head on up that road." He motioned with the gun barrel. "That's where you'll find your Texans. Remember what I said, now. Watch yourself."

Reeves stood. The two men looked at one another for a long moment. Haycock kept his Colt trained on the slave, his eyes steely-black and cold.

Bass backed a few feet, nodded to Wild Bill, turned and walked into the fog, heading north to find his Texans.

Staying close to the road, back in the trees, Bass trudged on; gone maybe a mile or two from where he and Wild Bill had parted. His adrenaline surge had spent itself leaving him weary and bone-achy. Decided to stop a bit, sat up against an oak and looked around. The fog had boiled off, the late winter sun starting to melt frost it touched. Quiet filled the morning where he sat. No birds sang, no air stirred, nor could he hear the sounds of any battle. Seemed oddly peaceful.

Closed his eyes to take just a couple minutes rest. When he opened them, a man stood over of him pointing an Enfield musket between his eyes. He'd appeared out of thin air, soundless as a breeze. It startled Bass. The man blocked part of the sun behind him, his figure a dark silhouette in the radiance, blinding details of the face. Glancing down, Bass saw moccasins with leather-tonged leggings laced up to the knees, what looked like a loose buckskin blouse. He appeared hatless, a cloth tied around his head. Filtering the sunlight, he could see wild tossed hair down to the man's shoulders.

"Where the hell you come from?" Bass asked.

"I reckon you should answer me that question, seein' as how I'm the one with the gun," the man answered.

"I'm, uh . . ." Bass stammered. Swallowing, he decided, no matter the fightin' side of this man, the truth would serve best. "I'm Colonel George Reeve's man; he with the 11th Texas Cav'ry."

"Then what you doing way down here?" the man asked sounding a little skeptical. "They's a piece up north of us."

"I's out fetchin' water for my colonel yestiddy. Got captured by a Yankee. He turn me a-loose this mornin'."

The man stood silent, thinking, still pointing his musket at Bass.

"Suppose I could believe that story," the man said after a bit. "Not sure why he'd turn you loose, though. We got darks back in the Nations on the Unionist side. How I know you ain't fighting for the Yankees yourself?"

"I just ain't," was all Bass could think to say. "You a Southern, then? Look here, you get me to my colonel, he tell you. Look at me. Does I look like a Yankee?"

The man leaned back, cocked his head one way then the other. "That's hard to say in this here war, but you ain't wearin' a blue coat, that's for sure. Well, I'll take you to *my* colonel, let him decide what to do with you."

They walked to a picket line a distance up the road. About a hundred men sat and lay on the ground, spread along and behind makeshift redoubts at the edge of the woods alongside a field. The road ran across one side of it. The fortification was more of a ditch with some rocks and logs hauled up in place. The men, looked to be mostly Indians, hunkered down behind the stacked rocks and logs. Bass's escort marched him, still at gunpoint, up to a squat man in a gray tweed coat wearing a Confederate officer's hat.

"Colonel Watie," the man said. Waited until the officer turned toward them. "I found this dark out in the woods. Claims he belongs to a colonel over in the Eleventh Texas. Says he was took prisoner by a Yankee, then cut loose."

The Confederate colonel had high cheeks, a broad face and nose, and bushy brows above deep set dark eyes. His weathered skin had a coppery brown color. Full black hair with streaks of gray fell to his neck. He looked at Bass; his gaze fierce, piercing. "Who's your colonel?" he asked.

"Colonel George Reeves, suh."

The colonel turned and looked down the line. "Can you shoot?"

"Well, yassuh, I does pretty good at that. Colonel Reeves's daddy, he—"

"Sergeant Muskrat, get this man a musket. Put him on the line," the colonel said to Bass's escort. Turning that intense gaze back to Bass, he said, "Today you'll fight with us." He turned and walked away.

"I ain't got no exter musket to give you right now," the sergeant said. They'd settled into the ditch behind a stack of pine logs where Bass's new comrade had led him. "We mostly all brung our own guns from home. When we get into the fightin', one of these boys goes down, you pick their piece up." Extended his hand to Reeves. "Name's Jimmy Muskrat."

"Bass Reeves," he said, taking the offered hand. "Who you boys anyway?"

"We's Second Cherokee Mounted Rifles. From the Territory. That there colonel you met is Stand Watie; he put us together back in the Nations as a home guard. We ain't supposed to be here, but General Pike he brung us over. As you can see, we ain't mounted, neither."

"Why not?" Bass asked.

Muskrat shrugged, looked over the top of the redoubt. "They got somebody else leading the cavalry. Guess they figured we couldn't do it. They aimin' to take them Yankee cannon yonder," he pointed across the field. "Might be your Texas boys. We're here to follow 'em in. Be comin' around them guns' flank whilst ol' McIntosh and his boys charges 'em head on."

Bass looked down the line where the other men talked, slept, smoked. Most weren't dressed much like Confederate soldiers. Several looked like farmers, many had on buckskins, moccasins, and the like.

"I believe they's going to be a lot of fighting here the next couple days," Muskrat said. "You bein' with the Eleventh Texas, I 'spect you know why we all here."

Bass shook his head. "Naw, I just goes where my colonel goes. I do know we in Arkansas."

A man came up behind them, and crouched. Spoke in a low voice. "Column of Yankee cavalry comin'. Don't fire on 'em 'til you get the word."

Muskrat nodded, the man continued up the line delivering his message. "Don't reckon nobody figured on this," Muskrat said to Bass. "This oughta be easy pickin's."

A double column, maybe thirty, forty mounted troops entered the clearing of the narrow field, trotting along the road. Showed no suspicion of what awaited them in the woods. Once exposed completely broadside to the Confederate line, the command was given.

The tree line exploded in musket fire and smoke. Horsemen and horses fell as lead balls ripped through flesh and bone. The young captain at the head of the column turned his startled horse toward the tree line, drew out his saber. Raised it to issue a command, but snapped backwards when a ball blew open his left shoulder, another tore into the soft flesh of his abdomen. His steed gave a short grunting scream when a ball shattered her left foreleg causing her to fall and roll across her rider. Cavalrymen turned to run, several more were cut down in their retreat. The remainder scattered southward at a full gallop.

As the smoke began to clear, whoops started along the line building into full-blooded war cries. Several men jumped the makeshift redoubts, and ran onto the killing field shouting out their high-pitched yells the entire way. More followed. Bass stood and watched, not entering the field.

Officers came among the men trying to form up the celebratory troops; their mounted colonel rode to the front of them. To their north, at the far end of the field, the boom and shriek of cannon fire drew everyone's attention. The colonel gave a command Bass couldn't hear. The lieutenants, sabers drawn in one hand, pistols in the other, shouted the orders to their platoons, one after the other. "Fix bayonets! Advance! Quick time!"

Bass could see a rank of gray cavalry crossing the field in full charge toward the front of the artillery, their rebel yells reverberating. The Second Cherokee Rifles trotted through the field, advancing a hundred strong, toward the left flank of the cannon battery. Bass came out of the tree line, followed the forward press at their rear, still unarmed.

At fifty yards they broke into a full run. The first horses of the cavalry had leapt the rails in front of the guns and sliced through the artillery men. The Second Cherokee followed on the left flank, overrunning the gun positions, slashing, bashing, shooting the cannoneers as they went.

Running forward behind the hoard, Bass emerged from a fog of smoke and found himself face-to-face with a Union soldier. An officer, just a boy, maybe twenty, still standing at his emplacement, firing his pistol all around him with deadly accuracy. Fallen Cherokees surrounded him, his neck and shoulder bloody from his own wounds.

Bass slid to a halt five feet from the soldier as the young officer swung the big Army Colt around aiming it squarely at Bass's forehead. Bass believed in that fraction of a second after their eyes met they both felt regret. The Yankee lieutenant pulled the pistol's trigger.

The hammer clicked against a spent cartridge. Bass lunged, grabbed the Colt with his left hand, and planted a haymaker to the man's jaw with his right. The Yankee crumpled to the ground out cold.

The skirmish ended in a matter of minutes. They had captured the Yankee battery. Bass crouched next to a cannon wheel, emptying the cartridge pouches from the senseless boy officer's belt and loading them into the pistol. He removed the belt and holster from Yankee's waist and strapped it around his own, stood to look for his comrades in arms.

The men, wild and out of control, marauded in their blooded passion, excitement of the victory building into a frenzy. Bass watched the scene in disbelief, shuddering in horror as one man grabbed the hair of a fallen Yank, drew out his knife, and sliced off the scalp like skinning a hog. The warrior held his trophy high, and screamed in triumph. Bass felt his stomach churn, watch three other Cherokees take scalps.

Several officers moved among the men trying to put a stop to the mutilations, but the Indians ran amok in their warrior fever.

A Cherokee leapt to the unconscious lieutenant still lying at the base of the cannon, and with a yell grabbed the Yankee's hair and raised his knife. Bass put a shoe to the crouching warrior's chest, shoved him forcefully away from the downed soldier. He moved to stand over the Indian, cocked back the hammer of his newly gained Army Colt, and shoved the barrel hard upon the Indian's face. "Leave him be," he hissed. The surprised warrior scuttled away on his hands and knees.

Through two days and two nights of combat, Bass stayed with the Second Cherokee Rifles, fighting alongside them in the fields and woods near Elkhorn Tavern. He kept the big

Army Colt he'd taken, and several Yanks took balls fired from an Enfield rifle he'd picked up.

His new found comrade took a wound. They'd made a stand in some woods when a cannon shot exploded high in the pines sending a foot-long wooden shard into Muskrat's right thigh. The battle had turned that night, and their general ordered a retreat.

On the long withdrawal down the Huntsville Road, a cavalry officer reined his black stallion to a walk beside Bass who moved down the road with the other troops. Bass had Jimmy Muskrat's arm slung over his shoulders, his right arm around Jimmy's waist, helping him along. Bone-fatigued and numb, Bass didn't bother to look up when the horseman came alongside him.

"Bass?" the rider ask.

The young slave looked up at his colonel. Comprehension so dulled by his battle-weary mind, he stood dumbly holding Jimmy, trying to sort things out.

"Colonel Reeves, suh. You ain't daid," he said.

The colonel grinned. "No, I'm not dead, but I sure as hell thought you were."

"No, suh," Bass said, in his exhaustion-drained voice. "I ain't daid." He and Jimmy looked at one another. "Not yet, anyways."

The colonel regarded the rifle slung over Bass's shoulder, and the pistol belted to his waist. "You been fighting, Bass?"

"Yessuh, me and Jimmy here and t'other Cherokee boys took down our share of Yankees. They gots better cannon than us, though. Reckon that's why the general took us outta there."

The colonel nodded, looking forward along the road. “Well, someone else can help that man. You come on with me.” He held out his hand to help Bass mount behind him.

Bass stood looking at Colonel Reeves, turned to gaze at Jimmy. “All’s the same to you, Colonel, I’d like to stay here with Sergeant Muskrat. He save my life more’n oncest las’ couple days. Believes I owes him some help.”

The colonel looked down at Bass, perturbed. “You’re forgetting your place, Bass,” he said. “You’re my boy. Now set that man down, and mount up. Shed yourself of those weapons, too.”

Bass stiffened, giving the colonel a fierce look, who returned his stare in kind. Finally, Bass unwrapped Muskrat from his hold and helped him sit on a log beside the road.

A young soldier behind them had stopped to watch. “Albert, you help Jimmy here,” Bass said. Unslung the Enfield from his shoulder, handed it to Muskrat who smiled up at him.

“You’s a damn good fighter, Bass,” Jimmy said. “You ever get over to the Cherokee Nation, you look me up.”

Bass nodded, not thinking he’d ever be able to do that.

Taking the colonel’s forearm to mount-up, Bass pulled back on it, and looked into the man’s eyes. “I fought me a Yankee officer fo’ this pistol. Believe I’s earned keepin’ it,” he said.

Colonel Reeves regarded his slave evenly for several seconds, surprise and anger etching his expression. Bass could tell the colonel didn’t much like the sass. He’d never once disobeyed or talked back to Marse George, but the fightin’ he’d just come through put a change in him; he could feel it in his gut, in the sound of his own voice. A voice that said to his master, this wouldn't be the time or ground to put him in his place. Still, Bass knew it wouldn't be allowed. Knew the colonel would want to deal with it sooner or later, that he stood a good chance of getting the lash.

Bass kept his defiant stare, though; deciding he had no apology, no regret, inside him. Since Wild Bill had let him go, since fighting alongside Jimmy Muskrat and them Indins, something had loosened in his mind. Could feel it, but wasn't right sure what to call it. Maybe it be courage, maybe foolhardiness.

With the colonel's grip, he swung up onto the horse's rump. The Confederate officer spurred the black, and they continued on down the road to retreat.

*Thing is,* Bass thought. *Wild Bill was wrong. Ain't no need t'be a dead man t'be a freed man.*

What was left of them moved slowly south, Van Dorn still trying to recover his army, get what boys he could well enough to march again, and fight. Everybody knew they'd be heading east toward the Mississippi any day, but they hadn't done that in earnest yet. Pike took all his Indians and headed back west. Talk had it part of their slow movement had been because General Van Dorn tried to convince General Pike to stay with him; that he'd cajoled him, ordered him, threatened him, but to no avail. There didn't appear to be any Yankee army chasing them, so the need to move east didn't seem immediate.

Bass could tell Colonel Reeves was still upset; the man would hardly speak to him, when he did it was gruffer than usual. Had taken to looking at Bass for long periods like he was studying him. Sure enough made Bass uncomfortable. He waited for the hammer to drop, as he knew it surely would, but still felt no need to apologize, in fact, his defiance grew as the colonel's stares continued. Bass decided that if they tried to put a strap to him, be harder to do than any of 'em supposed.

They camped along the Ouachita the night it all came down.

"Colonel wants to see you in his tent," Sergeant Major Beauchamp said to Bass. The sergeant major had become the colonel's aide after Lieutenant Mercy had fallen at Pea Ridge. Beauchamp had been a Ranger back in Texas; fought in the Comanche Wars with McCulloch. He was as tough and mean as a buffalo, just about as big, too. Tolerated no insolence from subordinates, especially negro slaves. He often made that well known.

Bass looked up at the sergeant major from the campfire where he sat. Knew better than to question the order, but the temptation arose.

"Bring that Yankee pistol with you," Beauchamp added. He smirked at Bass showing his tobacco-blackened teeth, spit to the ground between them.

Bass stood, coming face-to-face with Beauchamp. They both had about the same height, Beauchamp bigger on girth through the chest and waist. Each eyed the other with contempt.

They walked the twenty yards from Bass's campfire to the command tent. The sergeant major let the young slave enter the tent first, followed him in. Bass glanced over his shoulder to Beauchamp behind him. “You wants to see me, Colonel?” he addressed Reeves.

Colonel Reeves looked up from his table. Held a deck of cards in his hands, shuffled them three times before he responded. Looked down at the Army Colt stuck in Bass’s belt. Bass raised himself up to his full six foot three inch height; standing proud, maybe even defiant, certainly displaying no contrition.

“I can’t have you carrying that pistol, Bass,” the colonel said. “It doesn’t look good among the men.” He shuffled the deck again.

Bass stiffened, put his hand on the butt of the pistol, took it off. “I ain’t no threat with this pistol, Colonel, suh, ’cept to mebbe Yankees and such.” He turned to give Beauchamp a look. “Fought with the boys to earn it. Took it off’n a Yankee same as they woulda done.”

Colonel Reeves looked at Bass and sighed. “You know, I oughta have you whipped for sassin’ me back on that road, but I let it slide because you’d been in battle. And I like you, Bass. You’ve been a good boy for me and my daddy all your life. Still, I can’t have you talking to me like that in front of the men.” He gestured a finger toward the Army Colt. “And I can’t have you totin’ that gun.”

They looked at each other steadily for several long moments. Bass looked over his shoulder at Beauchamp again, who stood with his thumbs in his belt grinning back at him with those black teeth. Bass made no move to hand over the pistol.

“Understand your feelings, Bass,” the colonel continued. “Warriors for thousands of years have been allowed to keep the spoils of battle. So in fairness, we'll do a game of chance for that gun." He laid the deck of cards on the table.

"We'll cut the cards," he said. "You get the high card, you keep the pistol. You don't, you give it to me."

Bass looked at the deck of cards on the table, then the colonel. He looked back at Beauchamp one more time. The burly sergeant major made a fist of his right hand, cracked the knuckles of it in his left.

"You go first," the colonel said.

Bass reached, hesitating slightly as his hand hovered over the cards, picked up a third of the deck. He looked at the bottom card, showed it to the colonel – the queen of clubs.

The colonel nodded and smiled, reaching to pick up the remainder of the deck. He turned the cards over displaying the ace of diamonds.

Bass became immediately furious. "That ain't right," he said. "You cheatin' me!"

The colonel rose to his feet. "Sergeant Major, take this boy and put him in irons." He looked coldly at Bass. "You've crossed the line this time, Bass."

Beauchamp advanced on Bass, grabbing him by the back of his left arm, and reached around to take the pistol from his pants waist. Bass wrenched himself loose from the vise-like grip, shoved the big man back with his left forearm. He yanked the pistol from his belt and spun, bringing the barrel down onto the side of Beauchamp's head like an anvil hammer. The sergeant major fell like an oak, out cold.

Bass turned back to Colonel Reeves, reached across the small table and grabbed him by both lapels of his gray wool coat, pulling his face close to his own, the pistol still in his right hand. The anger in the colonel's face blanched to abject fear. He tried to cry out but his voice had become choked with shock.

Bass pushed the gun barrel hard into the underside of Reeve's chin, rage having firmly overwhelmed any cogent thought in his head. "I ain'tcher boy no more," he hissed with menace.

He pushed the colonel back to arm's length, balled his left fist and smashed it with his smithy's strength resolutely into Reeves' right ear and jaw. The man's head snapped back, and he, too, crumpled unconscious to the ground.

A shred of sanity returned to Bass's mind and vision, he began to shake. Thought maybe he'd killed the two white men lying at his feet. Panic overtook him, and he bolted from the tent, his single thought only to get away. He half-ran, half-stumbled to the picket line of horses, unloosed the first animal he came to—a mule. Mounting it bareback, he galloped off into the night.

After running the mule headlong for two miles, the amount of adrenaline rushing through Bass began to subside, and rational thought started to return. He slowed the mule to a walk, weighed his situation. Had no idea of his whereabouts, nor in which direction he'd fled. All he knew for sure he was somewhere in the hilly country of south central Arkansas, land he wasn't totally unfamiliar with, having spent most of his growing up years thereabouts. As a boy Marse William had brought him hunting along these parts of the Ouachita.

Old Mistuh William had taught him a thing or two about finding his way in the woods, too; about finding his direction, especially at night, now he recalled it. Looked up at the starry sky, and located the star formation they called the Big Dipper, then the bright bluish star the two stars at the outside edge of the dipper pointed up to. All the other stars moved in the night, but not that one. Stayed put right where it was while all the rest spun around it. Mistuh William told him that one was called Polaris, the North Star. It always stayed there in the north.

Young Bass shook with fear. Couldn't believe he'd done what he'd done. Now, here he was, a black man alone on a stolen mule, surrounded by Confederate soldiers, most likely condemned and hunted. Odds of him surviving more'n a day didn't look good, not even sure how to go about trying. Didn't have much of a plan, but remembered Jimmy Muskrat's words.

He wheeled the mule left and kicked it forward, galloping west toward the Indian Territory. He was terrified, yet exhilarated. For the first time in his young life, he was a freed man.

# Runaway

From an interview with Jud Coldstone of the Creek Nation—posseman, guard, and cook for Deputy U.S. Marshal Bass Reeves:

*Don't believe anyone come looking for Bass during those years when he was still a runaway. The thing was, during the States War and on after, Indin Ter'tory weren't a friendly place for most white men. Onliest ones ventured in was outlaws who figgered they'd take their chances on bein' skinned over bein' hung. They was a lot of colored men in the Ter'tory at the time, though. Some was runaways, like Bass; others called theirselves freedmen after Mister Lincoln declared 'em such.*

*Him and me first met up when he come into Muscogee Town. He was about twenty years, at that time. My cousin Sugar George brung him to my attention. I'm most parts Creek m'self. My pappy was a Kentuckian who'd fought with Zach Taylor down in south Texas. He come up to the Ter'tory after the Mex'kin War, and settled in with the Creek. My ma was a Muscogee woman. Pappy and my uncles learned me all their huntin' and trackin' skills, also those for whiskey makin' . . . well my pap did, not my Indin uncles. I passed a lot of them same helps onto Bass whilst he lived with us, but it was later during his deputyin' days that the makin' and sellin' of the lightnin' put us at odds with one another.*

*I couldn't stay edge-wise with the boy too long, though. The thing were, he saved my life.*

Bass rode the mule hard westward through the Ouachita range and on into the Kiamichi hills of the Choctaw land. He'd encountered no soldiers, Yankee or Reb, coming across those mountains in Arkansas, but he laid low just the same. Figured cold-cocking his colonel and the sergeant major like he done put a price on him. Just lost it when Colonel Reeves demanded he give up the pistol he'd took from that Yankee. Figured he'd earned keeping it, but not the colonel. He ain't never crossed no white man, but somethin' just come over him. All's he could think to do was runaway, so he stole the mule and lit out.

Any Rebs caught him, he thought, would as soon take him back dead as not; any of them Missouri boys on the North's side would likely string him up just for fun.

He and his mule plunged though hollow after hill after hollow of thick pine and oak and hickory set in thin soil atop tumbles and thrusts of shale and limestone bluffs. The mule being a mule pushed hard up the rugged slopes and down, giving Bass all he demanded. The animal was stout and determined, but even the stoutest has a point where it'll balk, especially a mule.

Bass's mule stopped at the base of one more hill the young fugitive slave wanted him to climb. The beast pulled up and quit. Just stood stiff-legged in the shade of the late afternoon side of that hill where a fast-running stream skirted it. No amount of kicking, urging, pulling, or cussing could make the animal continue. "Come on, mule. We can't stop here," Bass urged, giving the beast another futile kick to its flanks. A voice from behind startled him.

"Believe that mule's done for the day," the man said. Bass spun, snatching his Yankee Colt from his belt and pointing it in the direction of the voice.

A black man sat on a blue roan mare, calmly looking back at him. He was dressed like an Indian – buckskin leggings, a loose pale yellow tunic tied at the waist by a faded blue sash. A turban of red and white calico cloth sat atop his head. His face was broad and his cheek bones high. His eyes looked back with dark curiosity. He smirked at Bass's show of anxiety.

"You a run-away, boy?" the man asked.

Bass didn't answer, just stared back at the man, a look of defiance on his face. But the fear in his eyes betrayed him.

"You smart to throw out that pistol, son. Plenty men around here would lay ya out, mebbe worse; some might do it to take that mule from ya; some mebbe think you got a reward out on ya, mebbe a white man pay to have you brought back. They's other might shoot ya just because they don't want ya here."

Bass cocked the hammer on the Colt and raised it to the man's eye level. "You ain't takin' my mule, mistuh," he said.

The man threw his head back and laughed. "I don't want your mule, boy, and I don't really care if some white man's after ya. Y'all in the nations, Choctaw land to be exact. Ain't likely any white men gonna come in here after ya."

"You Choctaw?" Bass asked.

"Aw, hell no," the man said, looking offended. "I'm of the Creek. Headed back to that part now. Been over here on some bidness."

Bass looked at the rider, his pistol still trained on the man, yet with some uncertainty.

"Now whyn't you lower that iron," the rider said. "I ain't no threat to you. In fact, you get that mule movin', you can come along with me. M'name's Sugar George. I'll get you up to Muskogee in the Creek Nation. Lotsa other boys up in there like you. Creeks'll take ya in."

After Bass dismounted and coaxed the mule over to the stream to drink, he mounted up again, and got the animal to follow the blue roan and her rider. They'd headed off up a barely seen trail alongside the brook.

"How is it you a Creek man?" Bass asked after about twenty minutes. "You don't look like no Indin, 'cept for your clothes."

The man looked at Bass and grinned. "My momma is full-blood," he said. "My daddy was a slave; he run off and lived in amongst the tribe back in Alabama. We come out here when that damn ol' Jackson removed us. I'uz a small boy at the time."

They plodded on in silence for another half hour

"You got a name, boy?" Sugar George asked.

"Name's Bass Reeves."

"Well, Bass Reeves, mebbe we can make you look like a Creek, too.

It wasn't much of a town. A few wooden building alongside one muddy road on the banks of a river. Old French trappers had named the river *Verdigris*. The most dominant structure in the town, a two story stone building, sat at one end of the street. Sugar George noticed Bass's curious stare at the structure. "Federal Indian Agency," the Creek said.

A clamor of bodies surrounded Sugar George when he entered the town; lots of shouts and loud talk in a tongue Bass couldn't understand. A time or two Sugar George shouted something back at them. A man walking to the side of Sugar George's horse pointed at Bass, shouted something which made the whole group laugh heartily. Sugar George turned and looked back at Bass, grinning at him.

"What'd he say?" Bass asked.

"He said you looked and smelled like something even a starving coyote would avoid."

Bass stiffened and glared at the man. Noticing his posture, George laughed. "Don't take offense, son. He's right. We'll get you cleaned up, get you some fresh clothes. 'Spect you could take a bite to eat, too."

Sugar George looked at Bass as if he expected an answer, "Ain't that right?"

Bass nodded. "I ain't had much t'eat but a little squirrel the las' few days. Bein' on the run, can't say I thought much about bathin' neither."

"What I figured," George said. "Well, we'll get ya fixed up. You'll find us Creeks to be a friendly people . . . mostly."

George straightened, looking over the crowd. His search fell on a man leaning against a porch post of the general store—a short, wiry man wearing a floppy-brimmed black hat. "Jud, come over here," George called out to him. The man seemed to give up his lean with reluctance, started working his way through the crowd toward the riders. Two feet from George's blue roan the man stopped and looked up at him seeming somewhat annoyed, not having the same exuberance as the others in the crowd.

Sugar George turned to Bass. "Bass, this is my cousin Jud Coldstone. He'll get you settled in." He turned back to address the man he called Jud.

"Jud, I'd like for you to get Bass here a bath and shave, find him some clothes to wear, get him something to eat."

Jud stayed silent, studying the rider on the mule. Bass studied him back. He judged the fella more white than Indin.

"Well, King," Jud said after a bit. "I reckon I can get him a hot bath and a shave. Believe I could fix him up with a good meal. But I don't know about no clothes. He's a sight bigger than what most folks wear around here."

"Don't believe we can wash what he's wearin', Jud. Looks to me like they'd best be burnt. You do what you can."

Jud looked at Sugar George, then Bass. He sighed and shrugged, motioned to Bass. "C'mon then," he said.

Jud poured another bucket of near scalding water over Bass's head.

"Damn, man! You goin' to parboil me," Bass hollered.

"You got a lot of grit on ya," Jud returned. "Best way to get it off'n is with hot water and lye soap. You scrub yerself up; I'm going to go find ya some clothes."

Thirty minutes later Jud returned with an armload of duds—a buckskin shirt, a pair of blue wool pants from a Yankee uniform, and some long handle red underwear.

"Found these," Jud announced. "Got 'em from Charlie Three Toes stuff. He'uz bigger'n you, but everone else'd be too small for ya."

"Ain't that Charlie fella gonna miss 'em?" Bass asked.

"Naw, don't reckon so. He's dead. Kilt by a Reb up at Round Mountain. He was with Opothleyahola's Unionist boys."

Bass held the pants up looking at them. Nodded gravely. "I ain't never wore no Yankee's clothes," he said.

Jud shook his head. "Yankee, Reb; that stuff don't much matter around here no more. That's mainly a white man's war," he said.

Bass toweled off his woolly head and face. "You look plenty white to me," he said with a grin.

Jud nodded. "Could be mostly," he said. "My momma was a half-blood Creek; m'daddy was Kentuckian and a bit Cherokee. But he died fightin' some Pawnee on a buffalo hunt up in Kansas, so I growed up mostly with these Muscogee."

"But you that Sugar George's cousin?"

"Aw, hell, alluh us around here is cousins somehow or 'nother. You wanna get a haircut?"

Bass rubbed his beard and nodded. "I believe I does. Needs to shave, too."

"Well, get dressed then. We got an old man does that around here, if'n he ain't too drunk."

Jud handed Bass a length of rope. "Here, you can cinch up Charlie's pants with some of this.

"Best look back the way ya come ever now and then," Jud told Bass. "That way it'll look more familiar when you return. A trail can appear plum different comin' as it did goin'."

Bass did turn and look. They'd ridden over a ridge a hundred yards behind them descending down the groove of a deep hollow. The slopes on either side, thick with woods, inclined sharply. Oak and hickory, with a few sycamore scattered among them, reached bare-limbed toward the raw damp gray of the late March sky, but some swelling buds hinted at the approach of spring. A few redbuds had already started to tinge burgundy and pink; the bloom of the dogwoods still a week or so away.

"How far off is this place?" Bass asked. They'd already traveled at least five miles from town. Rode his mule, and pulled along another following Jud's lead. Two fifty pound sacks of corn grain had been strapped to the rear mule's back along with other makin's and some clay jugs.

"'Nother fifteen, twenty minutes," Jud answered.

"Why you put it so far out in the woods?" Bass's tone seemed to carry more annoyance than curiosity.

"A lightnin' still is something you want to keep well hid. Law don't abide spirits here in the Nations. The Lighthorse ever discover it, they'll bust it up and put you in jail. 'Course, not before they fill up they own sacks with what squeezin's you made. They'll say it be evidence, been my experience not all that evidence has made it to court."

"Why you go to all this trouble, if it's agin the law?" Bass asked.

Jud looked at Bass and snorted. "My pappy was a Kentuckian. He brung his recipe from them hills when he come west. It went back generations even before they was a States. All the way back to his great-great grandpappy who come over from the Scots.

"It ain't a matter of money why I run this still, it's family tradition."

Bass grinned. "But you don't give it away, do ya?"

"Well, I have my expenses. And there ought to be some compense for the hazards I gotta endure."

Jud reined up his horse and looked around, twisted in his saddle to look behind him. Turned back forward and looked down into a hollow that forked off to his right. After a bit he said, "I believe we's here." He pulled a bit to the right, urged his horse to walk down into the draw.

Jud dismounted at the base of the cut, walked into a thicket of sumac. From the back of his mule, Bass could see the form of an apparatus in the middle of the sumac. Jud walked past that to an overhang of limestone where the hollow ended in a ten foot high horseshoe shaped wall. Squatting next to a stream of water falling from the rock, he cupped his hands to fill them, and drank.

"Springs still flowin' good," he said. "Damn, that's sweet water." He stood and wiped his wet palms on his coat front looking out where Bass still sat astride the mule. "You might oughta get on down off'n that mule and start unpackin'. We gonna be here a few days. Makin' shine ain't no overnight thing. Not good shine, anyways."

Once the mash was ready, Jud had set Bass to splitting hickory and oak logs into sticks of firewood while he stoked the blaze under the kettle.

"First thing them fellas in the Lighthorse look for is a trail of smoke comin' out of the woods. String of smoke can tell 'em where a still's at. So it's good to have a thick tree cover over your still like we got here." He looked up and made a sweeping gesture with his arms. "All them branches spread out your smoke and not give any direct indication where ye be. Course, it's more better in the summer or fall. But that's a good thing to know just about any time you're on the trail and don't want nobody to know exactly where you are."

Jud touched his hand lightly to the side of the kettle and quickly pulled it off, then again, testing the heat of it. "Secret to good squeezin's is the right temp'ture to cook the mash. Cain't let it get too hot, or it'll be ruint.

In four days they'd completed the batch, filled up the clay jugs with ten gallons of high proof corn whiskey. Bass checked the load on the pack mule while Jud finished cleaning the still and securing it for another couple months of non-use.

"We taken another way back," Jud said as he came to his horse and stepped astride it. "Best never to follow a trail out what you come in on. You get into habits like that, makes it too easy to predict your goin's for them that wants to know."

They'd set up camp on a sandy river bank. It'd been late afternoon by the time they'd started out from the still, and Jud thought it best they use the next days' early pre-dawn hours to haul their goods to his place on the outskirts of town.

"Cap'n Sam Mossy Turtle of the Lighthorse has got where he watches me all the time," Jud further explained. "Well, most the time. Good chance he'll be dead drunk at four, five in the mornin'. We'll go in then."

"Think he watched you leave town?"

Jud smirked. “Prolly,” he said. “He likes to wait ’til I come back with some full jugs ’afore he arrests me. That way he gets the evidence.”

At dusk fire lights from the town started to pop up. Jud figured them to be a mile or so out, had turned to tell Bass that when three horsemen stepped into the light of their campfire.

“Evenin’, Jud,” the middle rider said. He was a big man and black with a pink scar that cut across his left eyebrow and cheek. From his seat in the saddle the man looked to be even bigger than Bass. Sat astride a large white-faced paint and wore two Colts strapped to his thighs, one of them he held unholstered, loosely aiming it at the campfire where Jud and Bass sat. One of his companions was a white man; the other an Indian.

“Glass,” Jud acknowledged the rider, a look of aggravation on his face. “Cap’n Turtle Moss send you out lookin’ for me?”

The man pushed the brim of his hat upward with the gun barrel, turned to look at the man on the left, then right, and laughed. The other riders joined in. “Last I seen Sam,” the man called Glass said. “He was passed out in the stable back of Dooley’s store.

“Naw, Jud, I’m out here on my own accord. Seen your fire, and come to investigate. I figured it was one of you whiskey makers.”

Jud stared at Glass, looking pissed. Bass looked on with uncertainty. “You come out here to steal my whiskey?” Jud asked.

“You got whiskey?” Glass asked. He got off his horse and came toward the fire. Motioning the pistol at Bass he asked,

"This that young nigguh run-away I been hearing about? The one Sugar George give ya?"

Bass stood, the fire reflecting in his eyes. "Ain't nobody give me to nobody," he said. "I's free a nigguh as you are."

Glass stopped and turned to look at Bass full-on. Sizing the young man up and down, he said, "Is that a fact?" He turned to look at the other riders, then back at Bass. "Well, out here in the Territory a man don't get free by running away and just sayin' so, especially no slave nigguh." As he talked, he walked up to Bass, stopping two feet in front of the younger man. The taller Glass looked down at Bass who glowered back at him.

"You got to earn that distinction, boy," Glass continued. "You got to prove you man enough to be called a freeman."

"How I got to do that?" Bass asked.

"Well, lots of ways, boy, lots of ways. It ain't just one thing. First I see for you is to take this gun away from me so's I don't kill ya. Course, if you do that, then there's my boys. You'd have to take care of them, too."

"Back off, Glass!" Jud said. He'd stood, holding his rifle by the barrel. "This boy ain't done nothin', he's igernant."

Glass ignored Coldstone, looked down at Bass's rope cinched waist where he had the Yankee Colt wedged. "'Nother way is you grab holt of that pig iron you got stuffed in your pants, and shoot all uh us before we shoot you.

"You reckon you be fast enough to do that, boy?"

Bass looked around, considering his chances.

"You could also try runnin' off into them woods, like you thinkin' now. You go on if you wants. I give you a minute head start. Course, that only show what a cowardly-ass run-away you really is. Once a run-away nigguh, always a runaway nigguh," Glass said. He turned and looked at his boys with a grin. They laughed on cue.

"Yeah, I 'spect you done some runnin' away a few times, yourself," Bass said.

The laughter stopped. Glass turned to face Bass again, his black eyes narrow and steely. "Make a move, boy," he said with flint in his voice.

Bass half-turned like he was going to head for the woods, then spun back lunging at Glass, but the big man was ready and agile. Glass side-stepped the charging young bull, grabbing him by the baggy shirt neck as he went by, and with a swift downward hack brought the pistol barrel hard onto the back of Bass's skull.

Reeves fell face-first to the ground, blackness swimming up to fill his sight, but somewhere in the murk he heard a rifle shot, then quickly a pistol shot in return. Just before the world went away, he asked himself, "Am I shot?"

When blurry consciousness returned, Bass didn't know if he'd been out for days or only seconds. The back of his head hurt fiercely. Someone rolled him onto his back and he looked up into the fuzzy black face of Glass.

"Stand him up, boys," he heard the man say.

He found himself standing, but not with the power of his own legs. What strength he had in them was loose and quivering. Two men held him up by his arms. He felt something smash into his left cheekbone and eye, followed a couple seconds later by a harder crash to his right ear, another to his nose and mouth, and yet another. Pain shrieked across his torn face, he could feel blood dripping from his nose and lips. His head sagged and he coughed. Felt his arms released, and he slumped to the ground. Tried to crawl, but something bigger than a fist smashed into the soft space where the ribs separated from his breastbone knocking the wind out of him. Tried to cry out but couldn't. Two more blows into his ribcage curled him into a fetal position. Gasping to bring air back into his lungs, he believed he would soon die.

He couldn't see out of his swollen-shut eyes, but he sensed the big man Glass squatting beside him. "We killed your partner, Coldstone. He was stupid, tried to shoot me," Glass said. "But I'm going to let you live, boy, because I want you to know who Dick Glass is, what I can do to you. You let other folks know what you got from me, that I ain't someone to be messed with. So I ain't killin' you, but I'll tell you this: if I ever see you again, I'll have Bad Horse here skin you alive, then I'll kill you."

Bass lay in the dying warmth of the campfire, unable to move, painfully trying to breathe again, trying to stay alive. He couldn't see, but listened to the clank and rattle of the mules being packed up, heard the men ride off. Presently, there was only silence of the night and seeping cold. Sometime in the darkness, shivering, his world went black.

Awakened, unsure if he was in hell or high water. The puffed lids of his right eye opened a slit, could see the glow of dying coals in the fire. Pressing cold gripped him like the hand of death. Knew if he didn't build back that fire and get some warmth soon, he would freeze to death.

Pain stabbed him sharply in his ribs as he push on the ground with his hands, trying to rise. A guttural moan shook from his throat. The shuddering cold drove him on, but before he could reach the fire pit, the agony became too intense, and he blacked out again.

The meager heat grew. Several minutes passed, maybe a half hour, before the fire began to shed the iciness from his beaten body. Bass opened his barely-seeing right eye as much as he could. Found himself lying on the sand, huddled close to the fire. Staying that way for several long minutes, still shivering as much with pain as the cold, he tried to weave conscious thought back into his foggy brain.

Questions arose: *Where am I? What happened? How did I get by this fire?* A man had beaten him senseless, came one answer, a face flashed into his mind: a black face with a pink scar across one side. *Dick Glass; said his name was Dick Glass.* But the fire? Remembered wanting to rekindle the fire, couldn't remember doing it. Some fuddled image of someone pulling him toward some flames.

"Jud?" he called out, but the name wasn't distinctive, only a fearful noise coming from his mangled mouth.

In a clump near the fire's edge, Bass saw his partner curled under his saddle blanket, unmoving. He managed to stand and shuffle over to the crumpled pile, pulling back a corner of the blanket. A curled up corpse lay on the ground pale and still; a blood-red hole in its upper chest. "Jud?" Bass called again. Put his hand onto his partner's shoulder, shaking it. The corpse groaned, his eyes fluttered open.

"Bass, you ain't daid?" Jud asked in a weak voice.

"You been shot, Jud," Bass said.

"I know. I built the fire back up and drug you over to it. Didn't know if you's gonna live or not." Jud gave out a rumbling, frothy cough. "That damn Dick Glass. Left us for dead and took our whiskey, didn't he."

Bass felt at his waistband, and looked around. "Believe they took my Yankee Colt, too," he said.

Another coughing fit racked Jud. “Reckon I’m a done; don’t think I can stand,” he said. “Bass, you go to them lights yonder, that’s town. Ain’t more’n a mile or so away. Find Sugar George, tell him who kilt me.”

“Naw, I ain’t leaving you here, Jud.” Bass slide his arms under Coldstone’s wiry frame and stood with him cradled. The pain at his ribs made him scream into the cold night. Bright spots flashed in his nearly blinded sight, and he staggered, thinking he would black out again.

“You can’t carry me, Bass. I ain’t gonna make it, anyways. Put me down.”

“Shut up, Jud,” Bass said. “You ain’t gonna die.” He swung his head around, and looking through the slit of his right eye, found what he thought were the firelights of town. With a lurch and a stumble, he started walking toward them.

Bass carried Jud up to the door of Sam Mossy Turtle’s jailhouse. He kicked the oak door with his bare foot, still standing there holding his partner in his arms. “Cap’n!” he yelled out. He got no immediate response, so he kicked the door, called out again.

He set the wounded man next to the wall, leaning him against it, then fell to the ground, the pain of his own infirmities overcoming the adrenaline still left in his body. His breathing was ragged and agonizing. Tried to call again, but only a whispered groan came out. Mustering his last bit of strength, he beat a fist against the bottom of the wooden door before the world went black again.

A Yankee stood over him pushing the spiked end of a bayoneted Enfield into his ribs, twisting it over and over. But the Yankee wasn't right, maybe a woman. Bass raised his arm to stop him . . . or her, but only brushed the air. Pleaded for the man to quit stabbing him, but the soldier only pushed his flailing arm away, said something he couldn't understand. Someone else—another Yankee? Couldn't tell, everything was blurred—grabbed his arm and held it down. Blackness...

Something wet covered his eyes, he reached up to remove it. Saw nothing clear, a form moved about the room; a woman, he thought. He was lying down, not much light, some kind of smoke stung his nose.

The woman walked over to where he lay, bent to look at him. Held out a gourd in one hand. "Can you see?" she asked.

"Some," he whispered. His voice rough, came out ragged. It surprised him.

"Drink this," she said, handing him the gourd. He complied, taking a sip. It had a strong bitter taste and stung his raw torn lips and tongue.

"Who are you?" he rasped.

"All of it," the woman said when he tried to hand the gourd back to her. He downed some more, grimacing. It also hurt to swallow.

"I am Blood Moon," she offered no further explanation, only stood and walked away.

"Where's Jud?" he called after her, starting to remember some.

"He talks to the spirits," she answered.

Bass's heart sank. "He's daid?" he asked.

The woman Blood Moon had walked to a fireplace, looking into a pot that hung over the flame. Took up a spoon from the hearth and stirred the pot, tore some leaves from a hanging herb, rolled them in her palms and brushed them into the pot. Didn't answer his question.

Bass let out a moan, a sob choked his breath.

Blood Moon looked back at him, then again to the pot. "He is between the worlds," she said without emotion. "Not dead, not among the living."

"What you mean?" Bass asked.

"He had not much blood in him when you brought him. Now for two days he has been meeting with the spirits. He and they must decide if he should return to the living."

Bass's mind buzzed, again he fell off a cliff into blackness.

Bass sat in a chair beside Jud's cot, watching him. His friend breathed slowly and evenly, as if sound asleep, which Bass guessed he was, only he wouldn't wake up when he called his name and shook him. Blood Moon said the old spirits wouldn't let him awaken, they were still discussing Jud's life, his return to it or not. So Bass watched him, hoping there'd be some sign of awakening. It'd been about a week.

"How you feelin' today, boy?"

He turned to see Sugar George standing behind him with another man. Had heard the door open, saw the light from outside blanch against the gloom, but thought it was the old woman Blood Moon. Sugar George had brought Jud and him to her the night he'd collapsed at Mossy Turtle's door.

The swelling around his eyes had mostly gone down, and he could see again. "Doin' good," Bass said. "Waitin' fo' Jud here t'come around."

The King nodded. "It'll take more than one bullet to kill, Jud. He too damn mean for just one bullet." He smiled; Bass nodded back, didn't smile.

Sugar George gestured to the man next to him, a white man with a star on his shirt. "This here's Deputy Marshal Ledbetter over from Arkansas."

Bass stiffened, looked uncertainly at Sugar George. The Creek leader caught his concern.

"Not to worry, son. Bud here's a friend of mine. I told him about your run-in with Dick Glass. He just wants to ask you some questions."

Bass stood facing the two men. The deputy didn't look to be much older than he was. "What kind of questions?"

The lawman and George exchanged looks. "Take it easy, friend," Ledbetter said. "War's over. Ain't nobody out lookin' for you, leastways not from Arkansas."

He continued. "I been after Glass for some time now. What he done to you and Coldstone can be added to his list, assault and battery." He nodded toward Jud. "Your friend here dies, we can add murder. That'd make his fourth . . . least the ones we for sure know of."

"Whadda you wanna know?" Bass asked.

"Well, which way you think he headed, if he said anything about that. Who was ridin' with him?"

"Two men," Bass furrowed his brow and rubbed it. "One was a Indin, t'other kinda dark, but a white man. He called the Indin, Bad Horse. Didn't ketch which way they left out, an' they didn't say."

George and Ledbetter looked at each other. "That'd be the Choctaw Grif Bad Horse and probly Thibodaux Rix out of Louzee-ana," Sugar George said.

"Believe I'd like to help you find them men," Bass said. "I can track."

Ledbetter removed his hat and scratched the top of his head. "I need to bring them boys back alive . . . leastwise Glass, I do. How I know you ain't aimin' revenge?"

"Well, Marshal, I sho' nuf be wantin' me some revenge, but I ain't aim to kill nobody. That there Dick Glass done took somethin' of mine. I just wants to get it back. 'Course, I'd like to leave him sumpin else to remember me by."

Ledbetter rubbed his chin and considered. "Hmm, goin' after them three, I could use another posseman, 'specially one with motivation. You ain't too busted up to ride?"

"I kin ride," Bass answered.

Dick Glass had gone to Texas following the old whiskey trail south, the one known as the Potawatomie. It snaked across the Arbuckle Mountains on down southeast to the Red River. Ledbetter and his posse knew this because the trail cut across Chickasaw and Choctaw land, and his man Arlo could speak Chickasaw and Choctaw. Dick Glass and his gang left a wide and distinct path. Word was, he was headed to Denison to bring back whiskey.

At the Red, Bass pulled up. "I ain't wantin' to go into Grayson County, Mistuh Ledbetter."

The deputy figured he knew why. “Ain’t nobody gonna bother you, long as you’re with me, Bass,” he said.

Bass shook his head. “I ‘preciates that, suh . . . jist the same . . .”

“Yeh, guess I can understand,” Ledbetter said. Bass had told him his old master lived there, the one he’d punched and runaway from back in Arkansas during the war. Told him about that, too. Ledbetter knew the man; he’d gotten elected to the Texas House of Congress.

The lawman looked around and sighed. “Well, I figure Glass is gonna follow this trail back up this way when he brings his whiskey. We could jist as well set here and wait for him.

“I’m gonna leave you, Willoughby and James here with the cook. Me and Arlo’ll scout on toward Denison. See if we can’t pick up Glass and his boys, make sure they’re comin’ back this way. Once we’re sure of that, we’ll head back and re-join you.”

That evening Bass sat by the fire with the other two men. The cook was off at his wagon. They’d gone off the trail, back in the woods, to set up camp. It was near dusk.

“Was you in the war?” Willoughby asked. He was a tall rangy man with a full beard and lots of hair. His eyebrows looked like a tangle of blackberry briars, and his left cheek poked out from a wad of chaw from which he’d spit juice about every ten seconds. Looked like he’d broke more than one horse. James was a fair-haired peach-faced kid, who kept quiet. Bass wasn’t sure if James was the boy’s given name or his family name.

"I's a slave of a Confederate colonel, but I did fight some. Got separated and ended up with Colonel Watie's Cherokees. Fought with 'em at Elkhorn Tavern."

"Is that a fact," Willoughby said. He spit into the fire. "Hell, we mighta shot at each other. I's with the 3rd Missouri. Don't recall havin' the chance to shoot no niggers, though."

"Yeh? Well, I shot me plenty of corncrackers. They was easy to spot."

Willoughby grinned and spit into the fire. "Them Rebs had more of you coloreds fightin' for 'em, reckon they'd uh done better. Kinda odd a colored fightin' with the Rebs, though." He spit.

"I's fightin' to stay alive, fightin' to help keep them Indin boys around me alive. Reckon they's doin' the same. Don't believe none of us thought about nothin' else."

The sound of wagons came from the trail, maybe two wagons or three. The men grabbed their weapons and slunk to the tree edge to have a look.

The wagons were filled with folks, common folks, farmers and such—men, women, and kids, lots of kids. Willoughby holstered his pistol, stepped from the trees.

"Evenin'," he said to the first driver, a stout man with a broad-brimmed black hat. An equally stout woman in a calico bonnet sat next to him.

Willoughby startled the man, but he nodded his head and returned an "Evenin'." The posseman could see one of the sodbuster's hands slipped around the waist of a 12 gauge leaning next to him. He reined back the team of mules.

"Where y'all headed," Willoughby asked.

"Camp meetin' up at Colbert," the farmer said.

"Camp meetin'?"

"Yep. Orta be a good'urn. Hear they's even some fiddles and such there. Be lots uh music and Bible thumpin'."

Willoughby grinned and slapped his knee. "Well, I damn sure would like to go to that!" He caught himself, and with a contrite look, touched his hat, said to the woman, "Sorry, ma'am."

There must've been a hundred people gathered near the tent. The womenfolk had brought food they'd spread out on tables—fried chicken, ham, roasting ears, baked taters, lots of pies.

Bass stayed back at the edge of the crowd, leaning up against a pine tree; a little shy about mixing in with all the white folks. Saw the three riders come up. No mistaking who they were. No mistaking that mean black face with the pink scar.

The men tied their horses to the picket line, went straight to the food tables. Bass figured that might be a good time to go look in Glass's saddlebags; see if he could find his Army Colt. Then he'd find Willoughby and James, and they'd take care of Glass and his gang.

Sure enough, Bass's Colt was in one of the bags. He checked the load, saw all chambers were still full. Rummaging around in the bag some more turned up the leather cartridge pouch Glass had taken, too.

Bass shoved the Colt into his belt, and turned to go find his companions. Saw Willoughby talking to the Indian Bad Horse over by a feed trough that had been set up for the stock, the two of them maybe thirty feet apart. It didn't look like a come to Jesus talk the two were carrying on.

Suddenly Bad Horse drew his gun and fired. Willoughby drew and fired back. The Indian flew backwards onto the ground. He didn't move. A woman screamed, falling to her knees next to a small body on the ground. Bad Horse's bullet had gone wide of Willoughby, struck a boy of about five.

Another shot rang out, and Willoughby slumped to the ground dropping his gun. Bass saw Glass standing at the food table swinging his gun barrel in an arc out toward the crowd who backed away from the gunman, terrified. The only sound in the night was the woman sobbing and screaming on the ground next to the shot boy.

"Drop it right there, Glass!" Bass yelled. Glass swung his pointed pistol over to where Bass stood, seeing the young black man pointing a pistol back at him from fifty feet away. Glass smiled.

Bass didn't want to shoot, because the meetin' tent was right behind Glass where people had gone to hide.

"Well, looky-here," Glass said. "If it ain't that runaway nigguh. I see you got your pistol back. That's good, that's good. 'Cause I tole you next time I see you, I'm gone kill you. Guess that time is now." He fired.

Anticipating that, Bass rolled to the ground a fraction of a second before Glass pulled the trigger. He had no choice, he had to shoot. Glass's next shot wouldn't miss.

From the ground he sent off a ball from the Army Colt, aiming low. He figured if he missed it'd go into the ground. He didn't miss.

The ball hit Glass in the left knee an instant before he fired again. The impact pulled his aim, sending the .44 slug into the ground a foot from Bass's shoulder, erupting a small crater.

Glass grabbed his knee, stumbled, and fired again. He missed again. He hobbled toward his horse, mounted and started to ride away into the night.

Still on the ground, Bass cocked his big pistol and took careful aim at the receding outlaw. Another shot came from near the tent, this time the slug thumping into the ground beneath his chin. Bass turned to look and saw the coonass Thibodaux Rix taking aim at him again.

The crack of rifle fire came from behind him, and Rix spun to his right going down on one knee. He tried to stand, but fell on his face, firing into the ground as he went.

Bass got to his feet and ran toward the fallen outlaw, keeping the barrel of his Colt trained on the back of Rix's head, but the man didn't move. He stood looking down at him, still aiming his pistol, breathing hard when a boot came into Bass's tunnel vision, and kicked the pistol away from Rix's dead hand.

"First thing you need to learn is to make sure the sumbitch can't rise up again and shoot you," said Deputy Ledbetter. He had his Winchester barrel propped on a shoulder. "Shouldn't never figure a man holdin' a gun is dead, even if he is."

Bass didn't respond, just looked up at the deputy, and continued to breathe hard. But did feel some relief.

"Glass got away," he said.

"Yeah, but I believe you slowed him down considerable. Believe that shot you made to his knee was pretty good pay-back for the beatin' he gave ya. Doubt he'll get too far."

He looked over to where James and Arlo attended Willoughby, who was sitting up. People stood around the bodies of Bad Horse and Rix, staring and talking.

"Glass got around behind us," Ledbetter said. "Turned out he didn't have no whiskey wagons. Took us an hour to figure that out and get back on his trail."

He looked to where the mother still wailed, a circle of women now around her also weeping, trying to console; a preacher knelt beside her with his hand on her head holding a Bible, praying softly and tenderly. Someone had wrapped the little body in a blanket and a man was carrying him to a wagon.

"Sure wish we'd got here sooner," the deputy said.

# Redemption along the Red

From an interview with Jud Coldstone of the Creek Nation – posseman, guard, and cook to lawmen of the U.S. Court for the Western District of Arkansas:

*I didn't die the night t'outlaw Dick Glass shot me, it were touch and go for a spell. Hadn't a been for Bass, I'd uh died out there on the trail for sure. Carried me all t'way back to Muskogee, even though he's beat up half to death hisself. Old woman Blood Moon worked her medicine on me and Bass. I think I's as much wantin' to get away from her potions and witchin' as I was to get well from that bullet hole in me. She just plum scares a person into gettin' better.*

*Whilst I's out—talkin' to the spirits Blood Moon called it—Bass took off with some deputies out of Fort Smith lookin' for Glass. They run into him at a town down near the Red, had a shoot-out at a camp meetin'. Folks was killed, even a young boy, I heard. Glass got plum away, but not afore Bass shot him in the leg.*

*Bass oncest told me the main reason he took that commission to be a deputy marshal was to go after outlaws like Dick Glass.*

*Bass went on to scoutin' for the marshals quite a bit after that shoot-out incident with Glass. Did his scoutin' mostly in the Ter'tory, even though some of them deputies ranged down into north Texas. Didn't like to go into Texas much, 'cause he figured he stood a good chance of getting' hung down there, his old master who he run away from still livin' there and bein' a politician and all. Still, he did make some trips down into north Texas. They was a gal down there he fancied, name of Jennie. Been a slave girl, like most darks back then. Lived on a ranch not far from his old master's prop'ty. That's how Bass come to know her; ever since they was kids, he did. Bass jist couldn't get her out'n his mind, so he tuck the chance of gettin' lynched to keep travelin' down there to see her. Well, I guess he done more than just see her, as she bore him a couple young'uns.*

*Livin' amongst all them tribes mighta been the best thing ever happened to Bass. Not only did he come to know that land like a cook knows his kitchen, but he also learnt to track as good as any Indin, and to speak passable in all them tongues. What tribes he couldn't speak in, he could sign. Believe most Indins thought highly of him, too, more'n they did any white man.*

*Bass was plum handy with a gun, both long'uns and short. Could knock spit off'n a fly's lip from thirty passes, with a six-shooter in either hand. Was just as good with one as t'other, although he never carried more'n one belted. He oncest said to me, a man must not be too good a shot if'n he has to strap on more'n one pistol. And I ain't never seen a man a more truer shot with a rifle than Bass Reeves.*

Riders approaching brought Bass to the cabin door. As he pulled a suspender strap over his left shoulder, he picked up the Henry with his right, jacked a .44 cartridge into the rifle's chamber, stepped outside.

The two men pulled up twenty feet from the cabin's front, staying in the saddle when they saw Reeves with the rifle. One a stout man with a drooping brown mustache covering both lips. The other lean and clean-faced, sat taller in his saddle than his companion. Both were young men, younger than Bass. Both wore tin badges on their shirt fronts.

"M'name's LeFlore," the stout one said. "This here's Heck Bruner. We're deputy U.S. marshals."

"Charlie LeFlore? Believe I heard of you," Bass said. "Don't believe I know Mister Bruner." He pointed the barrel of the Henry toward the ground, un-cocking the hammer with a thumb. His smile let the men know they faced no immediate danger.

"We heard of you, too, Reeves. That's why we come lookin' for you," LeFlore said. "Sam Sixkiller tells us you could track a dead man straight into hell."

Bass laughed a little. "Well, some leave more sign than others, but if Sam said it, I 'spect it's true. You needin' a tracker, are ya?"

"We're needin' to go down into Chickasaw land to find a man shot and kilt a woman. Couple whiskey runners we'd like to round up, too, while down there. Said to be south of Anadarko, down around the Red. Sam says you know the land."

"Red River country, huh? Where you're talking about is Kiowa and Comanche land, out west of the Dead Line."

Reeves paused to let that sink in. He continued. "Ain't many men your side of the law likes to go out there."

The deputies nodded and glanced at one another, keeping silent.

"I take it this man what kilt that woman ain't Indin, or was she a white woman?"

"Naw, a white man name of Bill Pollcott. Believe she were Choctaw, a whore. He beat her up, choked her dead when he woke and caught her stealin' from his poke. Still, law says you can't go around killing women, even thievin' whores."

"Believe that to be true enough. I require five dollars a day, plus expenses," Bass said.

LeFlore nodded. "Court'll pay the goin' rate, I reckon."

"One of the men you lookin' for Dick Glass?"

"We ain't got a writ for him, but I believe if we's to meet up with him, we'd want to take him in," LaFlore said.

"He's likely out that way. We meet up with Dick Glass, there's a few things I'd like to discuss with him before you arrest him."

"What would that be?"

"He oncest shot a friend of mine, stole somethin' of ours. Shot at me oncest, but missed and kilt a little boy. I'd like to see if I could get restitution."

The deputies looked at one another, knowing what Bass implied. "You boys come in and have some coffee," Bass said. "I'll get my outfit together."

They rode southwest for the rest of the day crossing the eastern foothills of the Arbuckles. A cloud cover faded the daylight sooner than the sun set, so they scouted out a campsite near a stand of sycamores that edged a wide shallow stream.

Darkness came quickly, but they had a fire before the last shred of daylight faded. Deputy Bruner broke out some hogback and beans. The clouds overhead had cleared by the end of their supper. They sat drinking coffee by the fire in the light of a full moon.

Bass sat with his back against his saddle, both hands around his coffee cup. Took a swallow before he spoke. "This here's Plenty Buffalo's land. He'll let us pass through, but he'll expect something for it."

"Who's Plenty Buffalo?" LeFlore asked.

"Kiowa chief. Kind of a temperamental feller when it comes to folks traipsin' around on his land," Bass said. "Believe I can convince him we don't aim to take nothing of his, though. Any his men comes around, you let me do the talkin'."

A faint bawling came out of the night, the mewling of a distressed bovine. Seemed to come from the other side of the grassy rise beyond their camp. Bass grabbed his Henry and headed for the rise. The deputies followed. At the ridge they looked down on a rolling prairie glade sloping away from them, its grass silver and indigo in the moonlight. They could see a commotion of animals some hundred yards off.

"Pack of wolves trying to bring down a yearling calf," LeFlore whispered.

"Looks to be about five of 'em," Bruner added.

"Six," Reeves said. Levering a round into the rifle's chamber, set it to his shoulder. With no more than a three second aim, he squeezed the trigger. One of the wolves spun over and didn't move. The others didn't seem to pay much attention, kept attacking the yearling. Bass repeated the shot, and another wolf went down; then another. The three remaining wolves stopped to sniff their dead, looking about with uncertainty.

"Git on outta there, now," Bass said quietly. Talking to the wolves as if ten feet away. "Leave that cow be, and I'll let you live."

The laboring beast backed away, turned to run. Their blood lust still up, the wolves pursued. "Dammit," Reeves uttered. His fourth shot brought down another wolf. Fired again, but the slug hit the fifth wolf in its hip sending it sprawling sideways with howls of pain.

"Dammit," again, sent a slug through the wounded animal's skull.

Picked up the last pursuing wolf in his sights and fired. Again, the wolf went down with a yipe, but struggled back to its feet.

"Goldammit," Bass muttered and fired again, dispatching the last predator.

LeFlore stood looking out onto the moonlit prairie, jaw dropped open enough to clearly reveal his lower lip below his mustache. The other deputy did much the same, both stayed silent. Bruner spoke first. "Damnedest shootin' I ever seen," he breathed.

"It were only fair," Bass said with a slight tone of disgust. He turned and started walking back down the rise toward the camp, pulling cartridges from his belt as he went and loading them into the tube.

"Fair?" LeFlore called after him. "You took down all six of them wolves with eight shots. And in the dark."

"Well, it weren't all dark. Had the moon. Wasted two shots, though."

LeFlore and Bruner could only laugh.

"You can Laugh," Bass said without looking back at them. "But I'm the one's got to explain to Plenty Buffalo why I shot his brothers. Takes great stock in wolves, considers 'em kin. Best we go to him, 'fore word gets back to him."

"We need to saddle up, go haul in that yearling and them wolves. If we take 'em to Plenty Buffalo as a gift, mebbe he'll go easy on us."

As expected, Plenty Buffalo was not happy; not happy at seeing Bass and his two companions ride into his camp, not happy at seeing the travois Bass pulled loaded with wolf carcasses, not happy to see the lacerated heifer they also brought along.

The three men rode through the camp with warriors surrounding them, children and women shouting, dogs barking. Bass pulled up in front of Plenty Buffalo's lodge where he sat watching them with a scowl on his face.

Reeves dismounted. He pulled his Henry from its boot and approached the chief, taking a cross-legged sit in front of him. He cradled the rifle in his arms, waited for the chief to speak.

Plenty Buffalo looked at Bass for several long moments, his companions. He studied the travois and its contents, and the wounded heifer.

"Are those my wolves?" he asked Reeves.

"Yes," Bass answered.

"Who killed them?"

"I did."

Plenty Buffalo pointed at the Henry in Bass's lap. "With that rifle?"

"Yes."

The Kiowa leader's expression didn't change much, only a slight more squint to his eyes. "Why have you done this?"

"They were attacking this young cow I brought you," Bass motioned to the heifer.

Plenty Buffalo didn't bother looking at the heifer again. "That is not my cow. I have no such," he said.

"I think the young cow was lost on the range, maybe from those men whose herds cross the Kiowa and Comanche land."

Plenty Buffalo said nothing, only stared back at Reeves.

"We will give you this young cow," Bass continued. "As a gift for allowing us to ride across your land." He waited a few seconds. "And the wolf pelts and meat," he added.

"We have know you many long times, Bazreef," the old chief said. "You are not look like white man or act like him. I think you are brother to the people, but it is not enough you offer. The wolves sacred. Their killing wrong. You must give more."

"What would you have?" Reeves asked.

The old chief looked over Bass, his hat, his clothes, his weapons. Looked out at the other two men who still sat a-saddle. Said something to one of his warriors in his own tongue and motioned with his hand. The young Indian moved to Bruner's horse grabbing a side strap of the bridle. Yelled something to the deputy, motioning for him to dismount.

Bruner looked confused and concerned. "What the hell does he want?" he called out to Reeves.

"I will take the gray horse your tall man rides . . . and your rifle," said Plenty Buffalo. "It is not enough, but I will allow it."

Bass looked at the ground, then up at the Kiowa with stern eyes. "Plenty Buffalo asks a fair tribute," he said. "But he knows I cannot give him a rifle. The soldiers will arrest us."

The Kiowa chief grunted in disgust. Looked above Bass's eyes, studying the scout's head cover. Plenty Buffalo pointed and said, "Then I will also take that instead."

Bass glanced up at the underside of his hat brim. "You mean my hat?" The hat was a water-proof, beaver skin Stetson "Boss." Bass had paid a pretty penny for it. It was his pride and joy.

"I have long admired this hat on white men," the chief said. "But never I would wear theirs. Yours I would wear, Bazreef."

Bass nodded and turned to Bruner. "Get down off your horse and take your outfit off it. Plenty Buffalo wants your horse, and we're giving it to him."

"My horse?" Bruner protested. "Like hell you are!"

Bass stood and walked over to the deputy, speaking to him quietly but sharply. "Bruner, you need to get down and hand 'em your horse unless you wanna get us all skint. We'll get you another horse, but until then you're going to have to double up with LeFlore."

Bass walked back to where the chief sat. "Plenty Buffalo is a fair man," he said. "We will give you all you ask, the gray horse . . ." He sighed and removed his Stetson Boss, running his fingers across the crown feeling the soft fur of the beaver belly leather one last time. Then he handed it to Plenty Buffalo. "And the hat," he said.

The old chief did not smile, but took the hat and immediately placed it on his head. Looking up at Bass, he said, “We will eat some of the wolf you killed to honor them. Do you have whiskey?”

Bass shook his head. “No whiskey,” he said.

The chief muttered something, gave orders for the women to start preparing the feast.

The trio left at first dawn, Bruner behind LeFlore on the latter’s horse, Reeves pulling the travois loaded with Bruner’s gear. They struck out to the southeast, heading for the place on the Red River where the killer Bill Pollcott was said to stay. Halfway there they crossed the path of a herd being driven north to Kansas. Bass knew the bunch and their ramrod, Bush Hamm. After Bass explained what they were doing and why they only had two horses, Hamm let them cut a horse from the remuda.

“Who do I bill for this mare, your boss or Plenty Buffalo?” Hamm asked. Then he laughed at the lawmen’s look of humiliation. “It ain’t nothing to be embarrassed about, boys. I expect I’ll have to fork over a couple horses to that old thief, too, before I can get acrost his land.”

At the trading post below the whiskey trail called the Pottawatomie they found Pollcott and the two whiskey runners. Unlike the two whiskey runners, Bill Pollcott didn’t go down without a fight.

“Bill Pollcott,” LeFlore said. “You’re under arrest for the murder of Wildcat Annie Hushushi. Cotton and Cud Moore you’re under arrest for introducin’ spirits into the Territory.”

Pollcott pulled on LeFlore at that announcement, LeFlore drew faster shooting the outlaw in the leg. Pollcott bent and turned some when the .44 slug slammed into his left knee. Cursed LeFlore, straightened, and fired back. The slug snapped wide of LeFlore's right ear by a good foot, and the deputy fired a second time hitting Pollcott square in the chest. The accused folded inward, arms flying out in front of him, the pistol leaving his grip, and fell onto his back with a thud. He twitched on the trading post floor for ten seconds, then ceased to exist. The two whiskey runners went to their knees with their hands raised, pleading for their lives.

After the smoke cleared, and the deputies trussed up the Moore brothers, Bass said, "You reckon you can find your way back to Arkansas? I'll see to it Mister Polecat here gets buried, I'd like to head down to Gainesville, seein's we's so close. They's a girl down there I'd like to see."

Bass waited until dark before riding up to the shacks at the edge of the field, stopping behind the one at the south end. Big Woody would be in there, eating his supper.

Had to be careful traveling around north Texas. Bass figured the Colonel had gone off to Austin to do his politikin', as he usually did this time of year. Some of Colonel George's people still remembered Bass.

Since that set-to in the colonel's tent the night he'd run away, Bass'd stayed wide of north Texas. All over a Yankee pistol Colonel George didn't want him to have, even though he'd took it off a Yankee fair and square at Pea Ridge. Busted the colonel and his sergeant major in the jaw, and took off; either that, or face hangin'. He'd Heard Beauchamp followed the colonel back to Grayson County.

Beauchamp worked for Reeves' and his neighbor, Denton, whose land butted up against the colonel's. He's a overseer of some kind. Colonel George were one thing, but

Beauchamp another. Been a Texas Ranger, fought in the Comanche Wars; Bass only knew him as a mean and heartless bastard. Man had a special hate Indins . . . and for coloreds. No reason to believe he'd changed much. No matter that Mister Lincoln and the federal congress had abolished slavery, old ways and old grudges died hard. Bass was sure Beauchamp hadn't forgot him.

Jennie lived and worked on the Denton land. She and the two kids still lived with her daddy, old Mose, in his shack on Rattleweed Creek.

His momma and sister still worked at the Reeves place, keeping their jobs as house help. Abolition of slavery may have been the law of the land, but in some day-to-day existences it was hard to tell the difference. Freed slaves could leave if they wanted, but where'd they go? And how? Wasn't much that'd changed from appearances.

Big Woody, still the Colonel's smithy, could help him get word to his momma at the big house without raising much suspicion. Jennie, he could sneak in and see without nobody knowing. Their shack was a ways off from the others.

Scouting for the U.S. Marshal's office in Arkansas had earned him a tidy sum over the past few years, he'd rat-holed most of it. Some he'd give to Jennie when he'd come. He'd found some land just outside Van Buren. Not much, but enough to start a small farm, maybe set up a blacksmith shop, so he bought the ten acres. Paid cash on the barrel. No house on it, but Bass could build that.

He had a plan. Someday soon, he'd move Jennie and the kids up to Arkansas. Get his momma and sister Jane away from the Reeves' place; maybe bring old Mose, too. Once they got up there and settled, he'd marry Jennie like she wanted. He'd get out the scouting business, settle down and farm, care proper for his family.

Big Woody came out onto the small porch, all six-foot four of him, shoulders to waist blocking the light from the doorway. Raised a massive arm the color and density of pig iron, holding a kerosene lantern in a hand as big and hard as an oak bucket. Squinting into the darkness, he asked, "Who out there? Whachoo want?"

"It's Bass, Woody."

Big Woody held the lantern higher and squinted tighter. "Bass? Whachoo doin' out here, boy?" Not a young man, Woody could still hoist the hind quarters of a mule with his back and shoulders, or bend a horseshoe with his bare hands. As a boy, Bass had stood at the smithy's side to learn the trade. Big Woody was the closest man Bass ever had to a daddy.

"Come to see momma and Jane," Bass answered.

"Why, they ain't here, Bass," Big Woody said. "They up to the big house."

"I know, Woody. I need you to go on up there, and bring 'em down."

"Why fo'? Colonel ain't up there, neither."

"Well, I know. But he got spies. Someone'll get word to him, or one of his bounty hunters."

"Ain't you heard, Bass?"

"Heard what?"

"Colonel Reeves is daid. Got hyderfoby from one uh his dogs an' died less'n two week ago. You can ride on up to that house and go in t'see Miz Paralee and Jane your own self. Ain't nobody there care no mo' if you comes around."

Bass was taken aback hearing about the death of Colonel George. Two men couldn't be further apart in living their lives, but Bass had known George Reeves all his life, and carried his family name. There was a touch of something at hearing about his passing, Bass wasn't sure he could call it grief.

"What about Beauchamp?" Bass asked. "He still around?"

Big Woody knew the history between Beauchamp and Bass. "Yeah, you sho' nuf oughta watch out fo' him. But he mostly over at the Denton place. They's runnin' cattle over there now, made Beauchamp the fo'man."

Bass thought a bit about what that meant. He nodded to the Smithy. "Much obliged, Woody." He wheeled the bay and spurred her hard in the flanks, heading away from the Reeves house toward the Denton ranch. His momma and sister would have to wait.

Woody watched man ride away into the dark at full gallop the horse at full gallop. "You watch out now, Bass," he hollered.

Thoughts fired through Bass's mind as he raced toward Jennie. Beauchamp was a callous and mean man. No matter what Mister Lincoln's law say, the law couldn't change what's in a man's heart. Beauchamp despised black men, held them in highest contempt, nor gave the least respect to the women.

Colonel Reeves had always been able to hold Beauchamp's smoldering hatred in check, but now that he was dead . . . Bass feared for Jennie. She'd told him how Beauchamp had come around, the things he'd said to her.

He spurred the bay again urging her headlong into the north Texas night.

Light shone from the cabin windows, but Bass could see no activity around it, no horses. He reined the mare to a sliding stop and flung himself from the saddle, breaking into a stumbling run to the door of the shack. Busting in, saw Jennie standing at the fire stirring a pot with little Robert clinging to her leg, crying. Six-year-old Sarah was at the table putting out the eating utensils. Old Mose wasn't in the shack. Startled, they all looked up at him with surprise when they recognized him.

"Bass," Jennie exhaled.

"Daddy!" little Sarah squealed, ran to him.

Baby Robert screeched, cried louder. Jennie unwound him from her leg, picking him up. "It's okay, baby. It's yo' daddy. Shush," she said to the toddler. "Heard you ride up. I thought it was . . ." She read the disquiet in Bass's face. "What's wrong?" she asked.

"I just seen Big Woody," he answered. Looked around the inside of the shack, stuck his head out the door. "He tole me Colonel George done died, and I . . ." He looked down at little Sarah who clung to his waist. He stroked her head. Looked up at Jennie, tear redness in his eyes. "I was skeerd for you."

Jennie lowered her eyes, turned back to the fire, stirring the pot again.

"Where's Mose?"

Jennie kept her back to him, turned her head slightly to speak. "He ain't come in yet. They got him working at the cow pens, but he too old fo' that. I's worried about him."

"The cow pens? Who make him do that?"

"It's that Mistuh Beauchamp. He say, if we gone live in this shack, all us gotta work." She looked into the pot again, stirred a few seconds and said softly, "Say, all us gotta do sumpin."

Bass pulled his daughter from his waist, looking uncertainly at Jennie. "What you mean, Jen. What's he done to you?" he asked. But she remained silent, stirring the pot.

"Jen?"

"You can't stay here, Bass. That Beauchamp, he lookin' fo' you. He know these your chil'ren. He know you'd be comin' back." There was real fear in her voice now.

"What're you saying, Jen? Has he been comin' around here."

"You gotta go, Bass. He be here soon. He say he gone hurt the chil'ren if I don't do as he say. He tole me he's gonna kill you if he see you."

The distinct click of a pistol hammer being cocked came from the doorway behind them. "Well, looka here," boomed the menacing voice of Silas Beauchamp. "If it ain't Colonel Reeves' runaway nigger done come back."

Bass instinctively started to turn and draw his Colt, Beauchamp raised his arm, pointed his own point-blank at Bass's forehead. With the other hand he reached out and grabbed Sarah by her dress front, pulling her to him.

"Go ahead, nigger," Beauchamp hissed. "I'll explode your brains all over this room afore you clear leather.

Bass tensed, then raised his hands above his waist, palms out, his gaze steady and steely at Beauchamp's eyes.

"That's right, now unhitch that gun belt and let it drop, then kick it over here."

Bass complied, keeping his body in a crouch.

Beauchamp put the gun barrel to Sarah's temple. "You try to jump me, boy, I'll take out this little bitch whelp of yourn before you can say scat."

He hollered over his shoulder. "Morchek, come in here!"

Another man came in through the door, his pistol drawn. Bass straightened some, kept the eye of the wolf on his enemy.

"Well this come out better'n I thought," Beauchamp said with a smile. "I come over here to tell the nigress ole Mose is dead, and here I find Bass Reeves. The nigger boy I been lookin' for ever since Pea Ridge."

Jennie gasped, bringing her hand to her mouth. "My daddy's dead?" she wailed.

Beauchamp looked over at her, a little surprised and annoyed at her outburst. "Yeah, he got trampled by a pissed-off steer." Then he grinned and said, "It was his own damn fault, though. He weren't fast enough to get out t'way." He and Morchek chuckled.

Jennie set little Robert to the floor, fell to her knees beside him overcome with grief.

"You let Sarah go, Beauchamp," Bass said. "You leave Jennie and the young'uns be. It's me you wants. I'll come peaceful."

"I reckon you will, boy. We got a rope and a hangin' tree right outside waitin' for ya."

Beauchamp stepped over and smashed Bass across the side of his head with his pistol. Little Sarah broke loose from Beauchamp's hold, and ran to her mother, crying.

Blue light flashed across Bass's vision and cracking pain roared through his skull as he sunk to his knees. Consciousness barely stayed with him, but he heard Beauchamp say, "That's for breaking my jaw back in Arkansas."

"Morchek, go get the rope, so's we can stretch this worthless coon from a tree."

Just as Beauchamp's man turned to exit the cabin door, an iron rod punched him in the forehead, felling him over backwards like a sawn oak. Beauchamp turned to see a black mountain of a man advancing on him wielding what he thought was a five foot long black saber. He raised his gun and fired striking his assailant in the midsection. Big Woody had already started the arc of his swing toward Beauchamp's head, and the impact of the .44 slug into the smithy's belly barely affected the iron rod's angular momentum. It struck the side of Beauchamp's neck with the force of a kicking mule, snapping it like a twig.

His vision still swimming, Bass saw Beauchamp crash to the floor. He crawled on top of him, drew back a balled fist with the intent to smash it into the man's face, but held it cocked. Beauchamp tried to suck in breath, but couldn't; eyes opened and glazed. Bass could tell, except for the spasms of the body beneath him, the man was already dead.

Heard a thud and turned to see Big Woody on the floor, his back against the wall by the door; the smithy's breathing ragged and labored. He gave out a faint groan.

Bass crawled over to him. "Woody?" he asked.

Big Woody looked up at Bass; eyes fluttered. Took a deep breath, licked his lips, and spoke. "I got Miz Paralee and Miz Jane out in m' wagon. It set . . . off a piece out in them trees by the crik. You take Miz Jennie . . . and them babies and get on outta here. You bes' head on back to the Ter'tory . . . where you got friends."

"Don't want to leave you, Woody," Bass said. "Takin' you with us. Momma know how to treat gun wounds." He looked down at the open red hole in Woody's shirt, could also see the spreading pool of blood on the floor coming from the smithy's back. "You be awright," Bass said.

"Naw, I ain't, Bass. I be gone afoe mornin'. Now looka here. You leave me with these two dead boys. Someone come here, they see it was me kilt 'em both. Give you some time to clear on outta here."

Bass put his hand on Big Woody's shoulder. Smiled, looked at him for a long time. "Woody, you the finest man I ever knowed," he said at last.

Big Woody tried to smile back. "Go on, now," he said.

They crossed the Red River at dawn, had gotten to Durant by mid-morning, and by noon, rolled up the road to a farm house northwest of the town. A man came from the barn when they drove up, an Indian—Choctaw, Bass figured, them being in that nation. A young woman was in the yard doing wash, a toddler played on the porch near her. A dog, looked like some kind of herder, lay attentively beside the boy. Its ears perked, he stood when the wagon approached, barking once. The woman turned to look at them.

Reeves pressed his foot against the brake lever, pulled up the team. "Mornin'," he said, pushing his hat back on his forehead.

The young farmer nodded, smiled back at them. “Mornin’.”

“Wondered if we could get some water for the mules. Mebbe some for us too, if’n you don’t mind. We driven up from Denison, women and babies needs to rest a spell, stretch they legs.”

“Course,” said the man. “We got lots of good cold spring water. You’re welcome to it. Come on over t’springhouse. You’uns can set in the shade, git out t’sun for a bit. Got some oats for your mules, too, if’n you think they’d take it.”

“’Spect they’d sure enough do that. I’m much obliged,” Bass said.

The man reached his hand up to Bass. “Name’s Whitehorse. Most folks calls me Davey.”

Bass took the handshake. “Pleased to meet you, Mister Whitehorse,” he said. “Bass Reeves. This here’s my wife Jennie, my momma Miz Pearlalee, my sister Jane and my two young’uns.”

“Pleased to meet y’all,” Davey said, touching his hat brim.

He motioned to the young woman hanging clothes. “My wife Atepa, and my boy Joshua.”

The woman smiled shyly, approached the wagon. “Would you like something to eat?” she asked.

“That’d be mighty nice,” said Pearlalee.

“We be glad to pay ya for a meal, and the oats,” Bass added.

“Nah, I ain’t hearin’ that,” the farmer said. “Git them young’uns on down out t’wagon, so’s they can eat. Our table is bounteous.”

"Well, we grateful, Davey," Bass said. The women and kids started piling out. Bass got down and unhitched the mules, leading them over to the water. Whitehorse followed along.

"Leavin' Texas, are ya?" he asked Bass.

"Yep."

"Where 'bouts ya headed?

"Arkansas. Got some land up there around Van Buren I figure to farm, raise some horses."

Bass's family and the Whitehorses sat in the cool shade of an oak near the spring house and ate their noon meal. The kids and the dog romped, the women folk chatted about this and that. Bass rolled up a smoke, leaned back to enjoy it. Watching the little'uns play, his boy and Joshua, his mind went back to the night he'd seen a little tyke not much older than these shot and killed. The incident had haunted him for years. He'd come upon Dick Glass at a church camp meeting, and called him out. Glass pulled his gun and fired, the bullet intended for Bass, but it had missed him and hit the boy. Even though the bullet was a stray, Bass had carried the guilt for the boy's death, 'cause he'd been the one started the gun battle.

"So you're a farmer, too?" Davey asked.

"Have been," Bass answered. "Done a lot of smithin', too. Works mostly as a scout for the law out of Arkansas. Figure on startin' up a new life for my family up there."

Several questions came up in Davey's mind, but he held back asking them. "I've farmed all my life," he said. "It can be a hard life; can't think of no other work I'd rather do, though. We got it real good here. The Lord has blessed us.

Bass snubbed out his smoke on a boot heel. “Yeah, I can surely see that.” He stood, looked at the hot sky. “Well, I reckon we best get on up the trail. We gots a piece to go today.

“Sure do ’preciate you and your missus’s kindness. We left Texas in kind of a hurry last night. Didn’t have much in the way of provisions.”

That raised more questions for Davey; still, he held them back. He stood, too, not looking Bass in the eye, but off to his corn field. “My daddy always told me a man’s bidness is his own to mind, so I ain’t askin’. I’d like to offer you some food to take with ya, and some coffee. Arkansas is still a good ways off.”

“Well, truth be knowed, we could use some of that, Davey. But I’d be wantin’ to pay you for it.”

Whitehorse shook his head, this time looking Bass in the eyes. “I jist can’t accept that, Mister Reeves.”

“Why not?”

Davey sighed, grinning back at Bass. “Wull, suppose’n you’s uh angel unawares.”

Bass threw back his head and laughed. “They’s several things I could tell you ’bout me might convince you otherwise; now my momma and Jennie? That’d be hard to argue, Mister Whitehorse, hard to argue.”

From a sultry morning, mid-afternoon grew to pasty - hot. Not more than five miles down the road the weather started to take a sudden turn. Big blue-green storms blew up and barreled down on them from the west stretching south.

"We gots to find shelter," his momma said. The wind turned cool, sending advance shoots of high altitude storm-cold through the thick sticky air around them. Except for that low hiss, everything had gone deathly still. A few distant rumbles sent warnings. All living things in the sky and on the ground had taken heed, had gone to cower someplace safe from the approaching wrath. The air made the skin prickle in an electrical field charged with primal fright.

Bass thought about turning the wagon around, heading back to the Whitehorses' farm, but he didn't think they'd have time to make it that far. Besides, they'd be heading back into the teeth of that storm, not away from it. He feared for their lives, being caught out in that weather; the air and sky had a taste and look and feel of a twister coming.

Bass spied a hill about a half mile in front of them. Looked like the only ground around that could possibly offer protection. He slapped the long reins across the mules' backs, urging them into a run, and looked up at the glowering squall line approaching from their left. Out across the flat plain, behind them, a massive wall cloud, as black as the halls of hell, had lowered from the storm cell. It moved in a slow rotation like the stir of the devil's cauldron.

"Heeyah!" he hollered, half-standing from the wagon seat, slapping the reins down hard upon the mules. Hardly needed to; the animals had their own heads, sensing the danger in the air. Pearlalee and Jane hunkered in the wagon bed each holding a child and one another. Squeezed the babies tight under their arms as the wagon bounced and tossed across the rough ground. Jennie, next to Bass on the wagon seat, gripped hard to hang on, looked terrified over her left shoulder at the green-gray monster roaring toward them.

Pearlalee saw it first. It started as an eddy of debris, tree limbs, leaves and hay, pieces of barn roof, there a plow and what looked like a barrel and a horse collar, all swirling near the ground. It started to fill in. Dark tendrils of cloud snaked downward from the wall base until they met the brown upward plume of rising dirt, all of it forming a wide snaking funnel, cloud-to-ground. Looked to be about a mile away, coming straight toward them, massive and death-gray in its roaring whirl. They could hear the beast's low rumble, like the stampede of a thousand buffalo.

Bass spied an outcropping of rock on the side of a knoll a hundred yards off to their right front, reined the team toward it, again giving the animals a hard slap with the leather. Closer, he could see an undercut of the earth beneath the layers of rock forming a shallow concave covering with an arrangement of small boulders at its front. A copse of trees stood some thirty yards to the front of the rock covering. Not the safest place for them to hunker down, especially with those trees so close by, but the best they had out on that open ground.

Bass leaned back to pull the mules to a stop. "Ever'one git out t'wagon, and under them rocks!" he hollered into the gathering wind. He stayed with the reins and set the brake, keeping the panicked team in place while the women and children clambered, half-blown, from the wagon bed and ran for the rock covering.

Handed the straps to Jennie. "Hold the team," he yelled. "I got to get them unhooked and set free!"

The back end of the wagon buffeted and the team stamped and grunted, tossing their heads and trying to rear. Jennie stepped over the wagon bench, leveraged herself behind it, pulling down with all her might, all her one hundred and ten pounds. Bass unhooked the trace of the left mule, pulled his knife and cut the pole straps. Slapped its hip, but the mule needed no encouragement to bolt. He moved to start unhitching the other, but the wagon groaned, started to rise from the rear. An ungodly howl surrounded them, a six inch thick tree limb, some eight feet long, slammed into the wagon side. Bass was pelted with sticks and small rocks and pieces of brush.

"Jen!" he bellowed. "Get out!" But she was way ahead of him, half leaping, half being tossed from the wagon bed. She rolled to the ground, the wind carried her along like a leaf. Bass scrambled after her, grabbing one of her ankles. Crawled atop her trying his best to cover her from the pelting debris and sucking wind, he could feel himself being drawn up off the ground. Grabbing at brush around him, he held tight, pinning Jennie as best he could. With his head fast against the ground, he squinted back and saw the wagon rise and fly away with the one mule, kicking the air, still held fast to it by the harness, then through the swirling haze of dirt and debris the vision of a large oak, three feet in diameter, came flying toward where he and Jen lay.

The tree smashed into the ground ten feet in front of them and skidded to a halt, the spines of its massive roots gouging the ground just a foot from Bass's head. More trees and parts of trees flew overhead smashing and piling against the jutted rock overhang where he'd sent his mother and sister and babies.

Then it abated, the funnel ascending back up into the cloud base, stillness descending into the wreckage around them. The tornado had died, but the rain started, coming down hard.

Bass pushed himself up onto his hands and knees, looked at Jennie. "You awright?" he asked.

Still terrified, Jennie nodded, then rose and looked behind her toward the rocks. "M'babies," she cried.

Bass looked at the place, too, now a jumble of broken trees and brush and other detritus, the front boulders virtually covered from sight. "Momma! Jane!" he hollered, rising to his feet and sprinting to the mess. Pulling at the twisted and splintered wood, he heard the children cry, first one then the other. "It's okay, Sarah baby, Robert. Daddy gone git you out." He tore at the debris, the heavy rain hampering his progress. "Momma?" he called out again.

"We here, Bass," came his momma's voice. "I think we's all awright, jist trapped behind this rock, cain't git out. Jane, gots a bump on the haid, but I thinks she awright."

Jennie had joined him, and they managed to clear a hole big enough to wedge them all out from behind the boulder. They backed up under the rock overhang, in amongst a heap of limbs and tree trunks which kept them mostly out of the rain. Little to no wind blew by then, allowing the rain to fall straight in its torrent.

They all huddled together waiting for the rain to pass, shivering from the cold rain, and their ordeal, thankful to be alive. They stayed in silence as the time went by, looking out into the downpour. Presently, it lessened, then dwindled to a soft patter. Bass stepped out of their little refuge to get a wider view, amazed at the destruction around him. A hundred yards away he saw the shattered wreckage of their wagon, the unhitched mule looking broken and dead still in its traces. Beyond that, maybe another fifty yards, he saw the other mule limping out of the torn woods, blood streaming down its hind quarter where a shard of wood stuck out of its hip.

Bass put the barrel to the mule's forehead, pulled the trigger. With no wagon, no provisions, no team, not sure what they were going to do. Only logical thing would be for all of them to walk back to Davey Whitehorse's farm, hoping they and it were still there. Even though only a few of miles, it'd be pretty rough going across the storm-wrecked countryside. Plenty of daylight still, but with the women and children, it would take a while. Didn't know what they'd find once they got there.

They set out, though, picking their way through the cluttered land. When they'd topped the rise in the road which brought them into view of the Whitehorse farm, they all stopped and looked. Jennie gasped, and Pearlalee put her hand to her mouth and said, "Oh Jesus help us."

xxMost of the barn still stood, but the house was a scattered pile of lumber and rubble. All the animals looked to be dead or gone, no sign of human life. The big shady oak by the spring lay split in two, one half having smashed the spring house. Bass remembered they had a root cellar, he hoped they'd gotten to it.

They found Davey near the barn, his head caved in. Alepa in the yard, just as dead, under a pile of broken lumber. Others came from town, they searched until dark for baby Joshua to no avail.

"A sad thing this fambly bein' wiped out. They was nice folks," Sheriff Ed Abel said to Bass the next morning. "We might never find that little boy. He coulda been blowed miles away."

"The Whitehorses have any folks around here?" Bass asked.

"Not that I know of," Abel said. "Moved in here a couple years ago from summers up north. Took over this farm from an old man lived here. Believe that was the boy Davey's onliest kin."

They heard a dog bark beyond the rise where the road disappeared. Bass and the sheriff walked up the rise stopping when they caught sight of the dog. "Well, I'll be damned," Sheriff Abel said with awe. Walking along the road in front of the dog, was little Joshua. The dog, muddied, limping from a front leg, and looking pretty beat-up, guided the boy along the road, touching him with his nose every now and then. The boy, naked and himself caked in dried mud, seemed okay. Later when they cleaned him up, they found some cuts and bruises, but nothing that appeared too serious.

They'd gone back to town, to the Baptist Church where a camp had been set up for other storm refugees.

"Twister must've picked that boy up and carried him away," the sheriff speculated. "Mebbe the dog, too. Anyway, I figure he somehow tracked the boy down, got him to a sheltered place to spend the night. Prolly laid up again the little feller all night to keep him from freezin' to death. It's a dang wonder he's alive."

Pearlalee, holding the scrubbed-up child wrapped in a blanket, feeding him some cooked oat meal someone had brought, said, “Well, whatever happened it’s a blessed miracle. Believe this little boy had the hand of Jesus on him yestiddy.”

“What you reckon’s gonna happen to this boy now?” Bass asked the sheriff.

Abel shrugged. “Prolly end up in uh orph’nige if they ain’t nobody takes him in.”

“We take him,” Pearlalee said. “He a miracle baby.”

The sheriff looked at Pearlalee, then Bass. “Well, I don’t know. He’s Choctaw.”

“That don’t matter to me,” Bass said. “I’s Creek.”

Abel scratched the back of his head. “Well, I s’pose if the council don’t object, we could allow it.”

“Believe we’d want that dog to come along with us, too,” Bass added.

# The Getaway of Cross-Eyed Jack Dugan

From an interview with Jud Coldstone of the Creek Nation – posseman, guard, and cook for Deputy U.S. Marshal Bass Reeves:

*Bass took his fambly back where he originally come from over in Arkansas. It were where his momma called home. Bought some land out around Van Buren, took to raisin' horses. His stock got a pretty dang good reputation, especially amongst them deputies workin' out t'U.S. Marshal's office in Van Buren. Bass would keep the best mounts for hisself, though, especially them was fleet of foot. He allus stayed on the lookout for some ole boy, citizen or outlaw, who felt he had a fast horse, so's he could race 'em and take in a few exter bucks agin that man's foolish pride in his horse. 'Course, most of them deputies knew Bass and still asked for his scoutin' into the Ter'tory. Eventually, when the federal court opened up in Fort Smith in the spring of '75, Judge Parker asked Bass to come on as a deputy marshal, which he done.*

The big sorrel was skittish, like he knew what was coming. He moved forward quickly in spurts, snorting and grunting, then stepped sideways until his rider reined him back. "Take it easy, Big Red," Bass said softly. "Easy. We'll get there."

"What's gotten into him?" Bill Leach asked. He sat atop the wagon behind Bass and Big Red, directing the mule in its traces toward their next stop. Bill's job was to cook, and drive the cook wagon loaded with provisions.

Behind him came a team pulling another wagon driven by guardsman Dub Willard; it being the prisoner wagon used to haul whatever outlaws they sprung up. So far, they only had a couple: one Bad Earl Thornbush, who'd shot to death a Seminole policeman named Hammetubbee, and Ada Maude Trotter who was wanted for hauling whiskey into the Territory, this being her second time arrested.

Posseman Jud Coldstone rode to the right of the cook wagon, slightly behind Bass and his big gelding.

Back in Muskogee, Bill Leach had been loading provisions onto his wagon while the deputy and his posseman had gone over to the Creek Lighthorse Police office. They'd gone to ask Sam Mossy Turtle if he knew the whereabouts of a horse thief and whiskey-runner called Cross-eyed Jack Dugan, whose writ Bass held among others. Bill had no way of knowing at the time that Sam was talking to Bass about a man named Shermerhorn, a cowhand down around Hellroaring Creek out in the Chickasaw land.

"This Shermerhorn, he rode with Cross-eyed Jack once. Might know where he's staying," Sam said. He looked at Bass, corners of his mouth turned up in a slight smile. "Also heard he's got a plenty fast horse ain't nobody beat, a gray pony."

"Who, this cowboy or Dugan?" Bass asked.

"Both," Sam said. "Shermerhorn has the gray pony. Cross-eyed Jack has got a big horse like your sorrel, only black and a stallion. He ain't never been beat, neither. Not since Dugan stole it, anyways."

"I'd heard that," Bass said.

Bill the cook also didn't know about all this back in Fort Smith when Bass first got wind of it. But it wasn't Bill Leach's job to know, just his job to cook.

"What t'hell's wrong with the deputy's horse?" Bill asked again. Directed his question to Coldstone after he determined the deputy wouldn't answer him.

"'Spect he smells a race comin'," Jud answered.

"What t'hell you talkin' about?" Bill asked. He had scorn in his voice. "Ain't no damn horse can smell a race." Bill was a querulous sort, not at all likeable; Bass put up with him as he was a tolerable good cook. Reeves particularly liked how Bill made the coffee and his blackberry cobbler. Out on the trail, you could overlook a lot in a man if he could cook good. Biggest problem was, Bill knew that, too.

"That big red gelding can," Jud said. "Only reason Bass rides him out of Fort Smith is to find a race. That horse knows it, too."

"Damn Reeves, always off wastin' time racin' hosses. We could get our work done in half the time and back to Fort Smith, wasn't for all this fool racin'." Bill didn't seem to care he was talking loud enough for Bass to hear.

Reeves reined up the gelding. They'd been coming up a gradual rise scattered with tall loblolly pine. The others whoa-ed behind him, waiting while the deputy sat in the saddle staring over the crest. A wide treeless valley spread before him down across a long grassy slope on the other side of the ridge. A mile or so off, the land looked smooth and flat except for a series of shallow washes along the middle where a creek cut through it. Bass could see a man on a horse working in one of the washes, clearing out a cow and her calf. Either the man was big, or the horse was small; Bass couldn't tell from that distance. But he could see the animal was a gray with white on its rump.

"Bill, you boys make camp here," Bass said over his shoulder. "I'll be back directly." He put his boot heels gently into the gelding's sides, coaxing him into a slow lope. Could hear Bill cussing behind him.

The cowboy continued pushing the cow and her calf out onto the open grass, keeping an eye on Bass as he approached. Reined back when Reeves got within fifty yards, pushed his hat up off his forehead, and laid his gloved hands one atop the other on his saddle horn, waited.

The deputy slowed the sorrel to a trot, pulling him to a stop five yards from the cowboy; kind of a scrawny fella, only about as big around and tall as a set fence post. Wore a stained high-crowned gray hat with a deep crease and rolled brim. Face lined and leathery brown set with eagle keen blue eyes. A thick mustache covered most of his mouth, a pooched-out left cheek told of a tobacco chaw.

"Evenin'," Bass said with an easy smile.

"Haddy," the cowboy responded.

"I'm Bass Reeves."

"Figgered you was," said the cowboy. "M'name's Elias Shermerhorn." He moved the gray a step or two closer to Reeves, removed his right glove, leaned from the side and stuck out his hand.

Bass took the handshake. "How'd you know me?" he asked.

"Well, I heard tell of ya. Boys in the bunkhouse talk about all the folks come across the range out here, 'specially you deputies. I seen that badge on ya. You being colored and all, figgered who you was. Ain't that many colored deputies, leastwise not your big. Folks around here knows about Bass Reeves."

Bass grinned and nodded.

Shermerhorn spit tobacco juice to his left, gestured toward the horse with a gloved forefinger. "Heard about that big sorrel of your'n, too," he added.

"What you heard?"

"I heard he was a strong racer."

Bass laughed. "What, this old horse? Well, he's been in a few races; won some, lost some. Pretty much past his prime now, though."

Shermerhorn shook his head slowly. "Hard to believe that," he said. "Sure a fine lookin' animal."

"Nah," Bass said with disgust. Gestured toward the cowboy's mount. "I bet that little gray of your'n could outrun him with no trouble. Looks pretty fit."

Shermerhorn laughed. "Aw, this old nag? She ain't nothin' but a cow pony. Traded her off a Comanche for a steer and two saddle blankets last winter. Felt sorry for the feller. Had two little tykes; looked to me him and his fambly's cold and starvin'. Believe they've et old Betty here had I not traded that steer for her. Comanch don't much like givin' up their horses, but I 'spect that'un figgered he could steal another'n.

"Naw, she ain't a racer. Don't reckon she could outrun even that cow yonder." He spit again, then squinted, Bass thought he caught a slight twinkle in the cowboy's eyes. "Nor that broke down old sorrel of your'n."

The deputy laughed, looked around. Took off his hat and looked up into the sky. "Sure is a fine spring evening," he said.

Shermerhorn looked up, too. "Yessir, it surely is."

Bass pointed out across the prairie. "This here'd be good land to stretch out Big Red's legs with a run. Been cramped up leading m'outfit all day."

"Yeah, old Betty could probly use some of that, too. She's been cuttin' cows since sun up. Getting' kinda stiff-legged on me."

"We could race 'em, anyway," Bass said. "Bein' horses, they might enjoy that."

"Well, I don't suppose it'd hurt nothin'," Shermerhorn said. Rubbed his stubbled chin with his forefinger and thumb. "Ya know, we could put up some money, just to make it intersting."

"You mean a wager?" Bass feigned surprise.

Shermerhorn nodded. "Do believe that's what they call it," he said with a grin.

"Well, now," Reeves reached into a vest pocket, searching; finding nothing, he searched the other. "Look here," he said, pulling out a coin and looking at it. "All's I got is this here twenty dollar gold piece. But I ain't sure I'd be willin' to lose that much."

"Well . . ." Shermerhorn drew out the word, scratching the back of his neck. "Yessir, that's dang sure a lot of money. Ain't sure I'd want to put up that much, neither, 'specially on old Betty here. Damn old horse." He started rummaging around in his shirt pockets and vest. "Hold on a minute. Got paid yestiddy," he said while searching. "Took in a couple poker pots last night." Pulled a wad of paper currency out of his shirt pocket and started counting it. "I believe I could cover that double eagle with some foldin' money, if'n you don't mind that."

"If it's U.S. tender, reckon it'd be okay," Bass said.

Shermerhorn looked out across the prairie, silently considering. "Aw right, then. Me and Betty'll race ya. But not too far a stretch. She ain't got much wind."

Bass nodded, looked out across the open land again, trying to suppress his smile. "How far you reckon it is to that big oak tree out yonder?"

Shermerhorn squinted. "I'd say mebbe a mile, three-quarter."

"That seem like a fair distance to you?"

The cowboy nodded. "Yeah, I 'spect so. How we going to start?"

Bass looked back at the creek, riding over to it. The cow and her calf stood at the edge of the water, drinking. He dismounted near her, picking up a fist-sized rock at the water's edge. "We can start back here. I'll throw this rock over my head, and when we hear it splash, that'll be our start."

"Fair 'nuf," said the cowboy.

Bass re-mounted and Shermerhorn lined up beside him facing away from the creek. "Ready?" Bass asked. Shermerhorn nodded. The deputy tossed the rock high over his head, but it had a narrow arc, and came down hitting the cow squarely on the back of her skull, then fell into the creek with a weak splash. The cow bawled, jumped sideways ramming her head into Big Red's rump. The sorrel screamed and reared. The gray and Shermerhorn took off like a rifle shot. The calf, bleating, ran in front of the air-kicking sorrel.

Bass neck-reined Red hard to the right and the horse wheeled, coming down with his front hooves narrowly missing the calf. Big Red neighed and huffed and pranced, confused and anxious, turning in a circle. By the time Bass righted him, Shermerhorn and his gray were almost a quarter of a mile toward the far lone oak, receding fast.

Bass dug his heels hard into Big Red's sides and hollered, "Hyah!" The sorrel came to his senses and responded immediately, digging his hooves into the soft earth and lunging forward, quickly flinging clots of red mud in a high arc behind them.

Bass loosened his control on the horse and gave him his head, leaning forward toward the rocking neck. Kept hold of the reins only for his own balance, and gripped Red's sides with his feet and thighs, praying he wouldn't slide off the hurtling brute. After two hundred yards, the rough ride smoothed out as the powerful gallop fell into a rhythmic glide. Bass felt the airstream around his face, his hat left his head held to him by its drawstring around his neck. All he could hear was the wind, the controlled inhale and exhale from Red's lungs, the cadenced thrum of hooves against ground. Ahead of him the small gray horse and rider began to get closer.

Still two hundred yards behind the cowboy and his little gray, Bass saw Shermerhorn turn and look back at him, give out a gleeful "Yeehaw!" The cowboy whipped his pony with the long ends of his reins. The gray responded with a burst, widening their distance by a length.

Bass, leaning forward nearly standing in the stirrups, half-yelled, half-whispered into the sorrel's laid-back ears, "C'mon, Red. You ain't gonna let that little Comanche pony beatcha, are ya?" To drive home his point, he dug his boot heels firmly into the horse's sides, and again hollered "Hyah!"

Big Red heaved forward. Bass could feel the muscles ripple through the power engine beneath him. The sorrel churned across the grassland like a locomotive, grabbing the red earth below his hooves, throwing it ever swifter behind him.

Eight hundred yards from the finishing oak, the big sorrel closed to a length behind the gray pony, gaining a yard with every stride. At seven hundred yards Red came alongside the gray, effortlessly driving past her. Shermerhorn's eyes widened in surprise. He whipped Betty relentlessly, and pleaded encouragement again and again. But the race was over. Big Red charged past the oak a good ten lengths ahead of little Betty, pulling away.

Bass reined the sorrel to a slow lope letting him cool off, get his wind back. He rode in wide circles around the oak. Shermerhorn and the gray came up beside them. The cowboy shook his head and laughed.

"That's the damnest thing I ever seen," he said, breathing heavy himself. "T'be honest, it's the first time Betty's been beat since I had her. I 'spected it'd happen sooner or later, but never like your sorrel just done."

Bass smiled. "Big Red likes to run," he said.

They slowed the horses to a walk. Shermerhorn reached inside his shirt pocket and pulled out his wad of bills and started peeling some off. "I don't never like to lose, especially where there's money involved." When he reached twenty, he handed the bills over to Bass. "But seein' that horse of your'n run, made it almost a pleasure."

Bass took the offered bills, and touched the brim of his hat. "Much obliged, Mister Shermerhorn."

Shermerhorn nodded. "Say, you're ever down this way again, you look me up. They's a passel of Comanches and Kiowas around here I can trade with for fast horses."

"Got a question for ya," Bass said. "You know a feller called Cross-eyed Jack Dugan?"

Shermerhorn looked at Bass a few seconds, gnawing his cud. He spit left. "Yeah, I know Jack. Rode with him some, worked here at this outfit a few months. Never did much like the sumbitch. Believe he owes me some money. What's he done?"

"He's broke the law; I got a writ here to take him back to stand trial in Fort Smith. You got any inklin' on where he might be?"

"Yeah, I reckon it's about time Jack went to jail. We never could prove it, but we suspect he stole some cows from my boss, Mister Miller. Well, last I heard he was over in the Seminole land, workin' on a ranch called the circle dubya. Hope you ketch the bastard."

"Oh, I reckon we will."

"Well, enjoyed the race, Deputy. I surely did."

"Me, too, Shermerhorn. Little sorry I took your money, though.

"Ahf," the cowboy waved it off. "Poker winnin's. Easy come, easy go."

The Circle W wasn't hard to find, but no Cross-eyed Jack. The foreman had fired him not two days before Bass came looking. Man didn't know where he'd gone, his best guess, he'd thrown in with a man named Isaac Gideon, who, it was said, ran whiskey into the Seminole land.

"Believe I'd look around Tishomingo if'n I's you," the ramrod said. "'Spect them two will show up there sooner or later. Ya cain't mistake Dugan. Rides a big black stallion. Says he got if off'n Indin, but I ain't so sure. And, course, he's cross-eyed as uh Spanish monk."

The deputy got lucky. Coming up a back trail toward Tishomingo, saw a black stallion, riderless, standing beside the road, reins tethered loosely to a low tree branch. Reeves halted his outfit a hundred yards back, rode up alone to where the horse stood. Pulled his rifle from its boot and dismounted quietly, looking around for the stallion's rider.

Back in the trees, some thirty yards, Bass saw a hat through the brush, low to the ground like the man was sitting . . . or squatting. The deputy circled around to his left, came up silently to the man's back twelve yards away. He could see the man's gun belt hanging from a tree limb, not out of the reach of its owner; man had his pants down. Reeves leveled his rifle waist high pointing it at the man. "Jack Dugan?" he said with authority.

The man started, but didn't rise. "Who the hell's askin'?" he responded over his shoulder.

"Deputy Marshal Bass Reeves, got a writ here for your arrest."

"Arrest?" Dugan laughed a little. Took a look up at his hanging gun belt. "Well, I tell ya, Deputy. You caught me in kinda uh compromisin' position here."

"You finish your bidness, then stand with your hands up. I got a Henry pointed at yo' bony white ass, so don't consider reaching for yo' handgun."

Dugan did as instructed and stood.

"You can pull your pant up," Bass said.

"Well, I appreciate that, Deputy." Dugan bent and pulled up his trousers and buttoned himself up, turning around to face Reeves. "What's all this about bein' arrested?"

Bass saw then why they called him Cross-eyed Jack. He advanced, pulling folded papers from his inside coat pocket with his free hand, handing it out to Dugan. Kept the Henry pointed. "Got one writ here to arrest you for introducing spirits in the Territory, 'nother for horse stealin'."

Dugan took the proffered papers. "Horse stealin'? What horse stealin'?"

"The horse stealin' that writ says you done." Bass took the gun belt off the tree limb.

Dugan held the papers close to his face. "Wull, hell, deputy, I cain't read."

Bass looked at him and smiled. "Guess you're just going to have to take my word for it, then. Now, let's get on out of here. I got my outfit down the road a piece. We'll set up camp and get ol' Bill to cook some supper, if he ain't too cranky."

Bill sloshed rabbit stew onto tin plates. Bass held one in each hand. The cook made no attempt to conceal he was pissed, but then, Bill was always pissed about something. The deputy carried the plates over to where Cross-eyed Jack and the other prisoners sat on the ground around the wagon. A chain ran through a ring on the prisoners' ankle shackles and up through another dangling from the wagon tongue. A padlock secured the two chain ends. Bass handed one of the plates to Dugan, took his to a stump some ten feet away where he sat to take his meal. Everyone ate in silence, except Cross-eyed Jack.

"Sure is a fine lookin' horse you got there, deputy," Dugan said.

Bass nodded, continued eating.

"He a fast runner?"

Bass chewed a wad of stew meat while he looked at Dugan. He spoke after he swallowed. "Tolerable," he said.

"You reckon he could beat my black?"

Bass ignored the question. "You know Dick Glass?" he asked.

"Who?" Dugan returned, taken a little off-guard. "Dick Glass? Yeah, I know Dick Glass; not good, though. Try to avoid him. Mean sumbitch. Why you askin' about Dick Glass?"

Bass stirred his stew, took a bite before he answered. "He's wanted, need to take him in."

Dugan looked around, whistled soft. "Believe you're gunna need more'n them two possemen and a cook to bring in Dick Glass."

Bass nodded and ate. Presently, he asked, "That black of yours fast, is he?"

Cross-eyed Jack brightened. "Ain't a horse beat him yet." Bass sopped stew gravy with a slice of bread. "That the horse you stole?"

"Deputy, I ain't stole no horse. Got that black in trade for a horse that was took from me. A colored woman name of Elsie Gilmore give me that horse to replace one her son stole from *me*."

Bass placed his plate on the ground, fetched his makings from his shirt pocket. "Yep, Miz Gilmore's the name on the writ who had that black stallion, only she claim you stole it."

"Well, I never done that. You find Sid Meechum, he was there when she give me that stallion. He'll tell ya I ain't lyin' and, by damn, she is!"

"I'll try to get a subpoena out for Mister Meechum. He can testify for you at your trial."

Cross-eyed Jack spat and swore, got all sullen. Set his plate aside and scowled at the ground. His expression refreshed as an idea came to him.

"I know how we can settle this, deputy."

Bass looked at him curiously, lighting his smoke. "Far as I can see, things is already settled, Dugan. You been arrested, and is going back to Fort Smith for trial."

"Let's race our horses," Dugan said. "You win, I give you the stallion; I win, you tear up them writs."

Reeves stood to re-situate himself, sitting again and leaning back against the trunk of a nearby oak. Took a long drag off his smoke and exhaled, the gray-blue cloud roiling about his head. "First off," he started. "What you're proposing sounds mighty like a bribe to a federal officer. Second, that black stallion ain't yours to bargain with."

"Awright, then, I got forty dollars in my bags. I'll give ya that."

Bass chuckled. "In case you ain't noticed, Dugan, that's still a bribe."

Cross-eyed Jack settled back against the wagon wheel, putting his hands behind his head. "Well, I thought you'd be a sportin' man. Guess you're afeared I'd put that sorrel of yours to shame."

Ada Maude Trotter, sitting at the other wagon wheel next to Dugan, hollered out, "If'n it's a bribe you's lookin' for, Deputy, I could supply you with a couple gallons of fine whiskey."

Reeves laughed in her direction, and said, "That'd be a mighty fine bribe, Ada Maude, if'n I's a drinkin' man. You know I's a Baptist deacon, ever touch hard liquor."

"Well, they's other things I can offer other deacons I know ain't never turned down."

She cackled.

Bass smiled and shook his head. Ground the ember of his cigarette butt into the ground, smacked the residual ashes and dirt off his hand. "Tell you what, Dugan, me and Big Red will race you and that stolen black, not for no money or anythin' else. Just need you to shut up about it. Won't be no need to tear up no writs."

Cross-eyed Jack grinned. "Awright, then. They's still some daylight, Reeves. Whyn't we do it right now?"

Bass stood. "Believe that'd be awright," he said. He stood and spoke to his guardsman, Dub Willard, who nodded and proceeded to unshackle Dugan. Posseman Coldstone, standing at the back of the chuck wagon drinking coffee, watched all this, looked to where Reeves stood saddling up Big Red. Cup in hand, Jud moseyed over to the picket line.

"What's goin' on, Bass?" he asked.

"Dugan thinks him and that black can outrun me and Red." He continued working on the saddle rigging not looking at his posseman.

"That mean you gonna race him right now?"

"Yep."

Jud sipped some coffee, looked toward Dugan carrying his saddle to where the black was staked. "You think that's a good idear?" he asked his boss.

Reeves continued with the saddle still not looking at Jud. "Ain't nothing gonna go wrong, Jud. You get saddled up, too; get your rifle. Set up out at the finish line. Dugan tries to run off, you shoot him. We'll tell him that."

Coldstone threw the remainder of his coffee on the ground and spit. "I don't know, Bass. Startin' to git dark."

"Just do it, Jud. This ain't gonna last more'n fifteen minutes. Got daylight enough for that."

"Awright then," Coldstone sighed, and walked to his horse.

The three plus Willard rode out to a space on the open prairie. Bass found a place he thought would be a good starting spot. Surveyed the dimming distance looking for a finish line and pointed. "See that clump of rock out there 'bout a half mile?" he asked.

Jud nodded; Cross-eyed Jack said, "Yeh, reckon."

"We'll run on out there, then circle around 'em and come back here. You head on out there, Jud."

The posseman spurred his horse, loping off toward the rocks. Bass kept silent for a few seconds letting Dugan contemplate the implications. Presently, he spoke.

"You try to run off, I tole Jud to shoot ya, he's a damn good shot. I'll come for ya, shoot you, too, as will Mister Willard here. I's shot felons attemptin' escape befo'. Reckon Judge Parker would see it that way, too."

Cross-eyed Jack nodded and smiled, said nothing.

"Dub, you set off to the side there and fire yo' pistol t'set us off."

Bass and Dugan held their mounts back, side-to-side. The steeds restless, prancing, making guttural sounds, fully aware of the game afoot. When Dub fired, the horses bolted without hesitation, the riders reining them only long enough to secure their gallop before giving them their heads.

Dugan and the black surged to the lead, but Bass wasn't concerned. Knew the powerful beast beneath him would gather and charge like a steam engine. At four hundred yards the black had pulled out to a three length lead, then four. Reeves spurred Big Red firmly, verbally encouraging a burst, and the horse responded. But the black steadily pulled away with no effort of a burst of his own.

At the rock outcrop turning point, Jud sat astride his gray and watched, holding the butt of his Sharps carbine against his right thigh, the barrel pointed skyward. Bass and his sorrel were barely distinct; Dugan and his black, an inky blur.

A hundred and fifty yards from the turning point, Dugan started angling the black to his right heading for the rise of a darkening grass-brown hill that made the eastern horizon. Jud shouldered the carbine, sighted what he could of the wayward rider. Leading the horse and rider, he hesitated, fearing he might hit the animal. "That's a damn fine horse," he muttered.

Through the evening air came the distant bellow of what sounded to Jud like his name; most definitely the deep bass of his boss's shout. Coldstone sighted again and fired, making his aim a little high. The report of the .50 caliber blast caused his horse to jump and turn. Jud turned in his saddle to watch his target, but the fading black mass of the duo never seemed to break stride. He extracted another cartridge from his belt, dropped the block on the carbine, and inserted the round into the breach. He again shouldered the weapon and sighted. Dugan and his black then nearly indistinct from the surrounding landscape, certainly beyond the reach of his Sharps carbine. He wheeled his horse and spurred her in the direction he'd last seen Cross-eyed Jack and his black stallion.

Bass, at full gallop, had heard the report of Jud's carbine, could see the bullet missed its mark. Gave out an angry "Haw!" and dug his heels hard into Big Red's flanks. By then Dugan and his black were a hundred yards ahead of him, pulling away up the slope of the hill. When Bass reached the ridge, he pulled Big Red up and searched the gathering gloom into which Cross-eyed Jack Dugan and his stallion had disappeared. Presently, his posseman pulled up beside him, and they both looked.

"Sorry, Bass," Jud said after a bit. "They wasn't much of a target to aim at in this dark, I sure as hell didn't want to take a chance on hitting that stallion."

Reeves grunted, continued scanning the nightfall below. "That is one damn fast horse," he saidt. "He was sure makin' tracks." Turning the sorrel, he rode back in the direction of camp.

Jud continued looking into the increasing darkness. He hollered back to the deputy, "That bein' the case, figure it won't be much trouble to find him tomorruh."

Jud was right. The tracks of the black stood out, and seemed to lead right into Tishomingo. Funny that Cross-eyed Jack would want to go there, it being the most obvious place Reeves would look for him. They got into town about noon. Bill Leach and Dub took the wagons over to the mercantile to pick up supplies, while Bass and Jud headed for the livery to have a look around. Ada Maude claimed she needed some salts for a gastric condition, and Bad Earl, complaining of a tooth ache, insisted on seeing a barber.

"Yeah, he come in here, that cross-eyed sumbitch," the livery man said. "Got me up outta bed 'bout two this mornin'. Rubbed down that stallion hisself—damn fine horse—and fed him some oats. Ast if'n he could bed down in the stall, which I said I'd let him do fer another two bits. When I come back in here at six, he'd already left out. Musta figured you's comin'. Sumbitch never paid me, neither. I damn well should've knowed better, 'cause I know Jack and what he's like."

"You got any idea which way he headed," Bass asked.

"Not fer certain, but, you know, now that I think about it, they was somethin'. One evenin' a week or so ago him and me was out front sittin' on some barrels; just enjoyin' the fine spring evenin' sittin' there talkin' like ya do sometimes. Well, we's discussin' how tough times was and how hard it were to make a livin' and all that, and he claimed he'd knew about a cave called Robbers Cave back in them Arbuckle Mountains up around the town of Sulfur. Said he knowed for a fact outlaws and such had stashed some of their loot back in that cave, some of which is now dead. Said one of these days he's gonna go up there and help hisself to some of that loot.

"I did notice him lookin' kinda anxious last night. Makes sense why he lit out so early, now that you come lookin' for him. Might be he figured that day had come, to go find some of that loot, I mean."

Bass nodded to the livery man. "'Preciate your cooperation." Mounted up to go fetch Bill, Dub, and the prisoners.

"I know about that cave," Bass said to Jud. They'd waited for Bad Earl to get his tooth pulled, then headed on up the road toward Sulfur. "Even been up there to get me a scalawag or two. Good place for outlaws to go to hide, at least it used to be. Ain't so well hid from the law anymore. Don't know about any loot hid there, though. S'pose they could be. Them caves is deep. Feller could get back in there under them hills, and never find his way out."

Some five miles south of Sulfur, they turned off the road onto a trail that wandered up into the Arbuckles. Woods got thicker the further they went, the trail narrower, the land steeper. They'd come to a glade, maybe thirty yards wide, with a creek cascading down one side.

"Bill, you and Dub pull up here, get us a camp set up. Don't believe we can take the wagons in much further. 'Sides, you're slowing us down. Jud and me will head on up the mountain. Figure we'll be back afore dark."

They climbed a narrow trail around granite shelves and ancient glacier-rolled boulders, through stands of loblolly pines, over a high brushy ridge and down into a valley cut by a clear cold stream. Followed the swift water downstream until they came to a wide bend where the water ran deeper and slower. Up along one bank, behind a stand of sycamores, a bench of layered rock jutted out from the incline. Under the bench a wide dark hole of a cave opened in the hillside like the maw of some angry underworld beast.

At the edge of the stream a black stallion, still saddled, the reins from its bridle dangling in the water, raised his head to look across the stream at the riders.

"'Pears Dugan's around here somewheres," the posseman said.

"Don't look like that horse has been attended to for a while," Bass said.

They crossed the stream, water coming up to their horses bellies. Jud approached the stallion which balked and shied. The posseman whispered him down, grabbed the loose reins and calmed the animal. Bass went to the cave entrance, squatted and looked into the dark chamber. He could not see nor hear anyone.

"Dugan?" he called out. Waited thirty seconds, got no response.

Entering the cave, he walked to a cold fire pit. Trash and debris around the pit showed humans had been there, but not lately. At the wall near the pit, he saw two inch-thick hackberry limbs about three feet long with pitch-dipped burlap twisted around one end. He took out a match and struck it, lighting one of the torches, picked up another, and carried it unlit in his other hand.

Fifty yards into the cave it narrowed, the tunnel curving off to the left and down, then back to the right after another thirty yards. Three feet out from the yellow glow of his torch's fire, pitch blackness surrounded him except where the flame reflected off the damp yellow-brown walls. He continued down the tunnel now lowering to six inches below his standing height. His boot toe hit a fist-sized rock, kicking it forward; he listened to the echoing knock as it rolled forward and down along the slope of a rock face, ending in a distant splash as it fell into water. Bass stopped and held the torch out in front of him. All he could see was the face of smooth rock falling off into a pit of darkness. Out of the corner of his eye the light caught something, and he shifted the torchlight toward it. A hat lay at the edge of the precipice. Reeves thought he recognized it as Dugan's. He kicked another rock into the void, counting to five before he heard the splash.

"Dugan?" he called out again, but got back only his echo.

"Dugan, if you're down there let me hear you. We'll get you out."

Still nothing. The deputy held the torch up high, first to the right, then the left, looking for any other possible way around the cavern, but as far as he could see the walls were sheer, the drop severe. He lit the other torch he held with the flame of the first, then threw it over the edge watching its foot-long flame spiral down into the dark until it extinguished with a faint hiss when it hit the water. Bass figured that to be a good fifty feet below.

He stood looking down into the nothingness another ten seconds or so, turned to make his way back to the cave entrance. The posseman waited outside the cave mouth with the black stallion.

"Believe he's in there, awright," Reeves said. "But ain't so sure he's comin' out, least not this way."

He looked up at the long shadows on the side of the mountain above them. "Best we get on back to the wagons," he said.

Cross-eyed Jack had slipped and started to slide. He'd been holding the torch high looking up to try to see the cavern ceiling when he'd come to the slope. He'd gone down hard on his hip and side, sliding out of control. The torch left his hand falling off in front of him as he tried desperately to find a purchase on the slick rock surface. His right boot heel caught on something turning his foot, sole-first, toward his face. At first, he heard, more than felt, the snap of bones. Then he was falling into the darkness, it seemed almost floating as in a dream, but his smack chest-first into water just a shade south of ice took away any thought of a dream. Sank a foot or two into it, then came to the surface gasping, not able to touch any bottom with his feet. He thrashed and paddled across the dark water hoping to find a shore. Presently, he touched rock, felt a shelf maybe wide enough to pull himself up on to. When he tried, his right leg stabbed him with pain. He screamed out, falling back into the water.

He managed to get most of himself up onto the narrow shelf where he waited for the pain in his leg to subside. Sat there shivering, as much in agony from his broken leg as the icy wetness that soaked him. Looked around and up, but there wasn't much for him to see. When his eyes adjusted some, he thought he could make out a spot of light above and to his left. Looked to be daylight, but how to get to it. He could see an outcrop of rock on the wall maybe four feet above him. With his leg, climbing would be hard, but if he could reach it maybe he'd find a way up to that opening.

Up on the shelf, standing on one leg, Dugan jumped to reach the outcropping, but his fingers slipped from it and again he fell back into the water. His leg hurt, but not so much as before; the water didn't seem so cold. Pulled himself up onto the shelf again and out of the water to his waist. Breathing hard, thought he would rest a bit, then try again.

Did someone call his name? Wasn't sure. He laughed. Sounded like his pa; he allowed as how he didn't never want to see that mean sumbitch again. Didn't really matter, though; his old man been dead for twenty years. Most likely it were that damn deputy still chasin' after him. He laughed again, a shuddering quick thing coming out between rattling teeth.

He looked up at the spot of daylight to make sure it was still there. Grogginess dragged at him. Noticed his leg didn't hurt at all no more; as a matter of fact, couldn't feel narry one of 'em. Thought he'd just take a little nap to get some energy, then with his broke leg all numb-like, he'd be able to climb on up to that daylight and get away.

# The Reluctant Posseman

From an interview with Jud Coldstone of the Creek Nation:

*They was times I didn't ride with Bass as his posseman out of Fort Smith. Not often, but times. One such I's laid up with a mule kick. Damn jackass caught me in the hip when I weren't payin' attention, and put me on a crutch and that Creek witch Blood Moon's poultices for two weeks.*

*Anyhow, I couldn't ride, so the deputy lit a shuck without me, tookin' just Bill Leach, the cook, and Willie Jumps-a-Creek, as his guard and to drive the prisoner wagon. Said he thought he could get along without me as Willie was a Cheyenne boy who knew the country where they was headed, Bass figgered that's all he needed. Musta plum forgot his need for someone to read his writs, which Bass could not do, nor Bill and Willie could do narry, neither.*

*Bass was headed for out west of the Dead Line that time I was mule-kicked, and left me b'hind.*

The ferryman, Orrin Paulette, had already started his pull to take the barge to the west side of the Washita when Bass and his outfit rolled up to the landing. Wasn't more than about forty, fifty feet out when Bass hailed him.

They'd left their camp near Anadarko at four that morning, Bass wanting to make the ferry crossing before noon as he needed to get west of the Dead Line, conduct his business and back across before sundown. He was hunting the Bruner brothers, thought it'd be best to meet up with them in broad daylight. Figured that'd improve his chances at staying alive. The longer he rode out from Fort Smith, the more he started to second guess himself about not taking along a posseman. Although it could be said the Bruner brothers were several kernels short of a roastin' ear, they'd still have him out-gunned three to one. Them boys might come up short on smarts, but a nest of cottonmouths don't need to be smart to kill you, just mean.

Bass lifted his watch from a front vest pocket, flipped open the cover. Already past eleven; if they had to wait for the ferry to cross and return, that'd cost them at least another hour.

The deputy cupped his hands around his mouth. "Paulette!" he hollered. The ferryman looked back at him and waved.

"Pull 'er back over here! I can't wait for you to go over and back! I got urgent bidness out around Fort Cobb!"

The ferryman nodded and waved again, moving to the other end of the barge, started pulling it back toward the east landing. One of his passengers watched it all with unease. J. L. Hoyt recognized Reeves, and wanted no part of riding the ferry across the river with him. He moved over to Paulette.

"What'er you doin', Orrin? You can't go back onest you started acrost," Hoyt protested.

"Says you," Paulette answered. Continued pulling the rope, gesturing with his head. "That there's a Deputy U.S. Marshal."

Hoyt's brow wrinkled, he sent a brown spit into the brown river. "Yeah, I know who he is."

"Believe his wants is bigger than your'n," the ferryman added.

Bill Leach rolled the chow wagon onto the barge, followed by Willie Jumps-a-Creek with the empty prisoner wagon. Bass brought up the rear. He surveyed the other ferry passengers: a freight wagon with a driver and shotgun rider, a fat-bellied Indian—looked to be Comanche—with two women, and a skinny white man standing next to a saddled mule. The deputy dismounted, started adjusting his saddle.

Hoyt led his mule to the far end of the barge, away from Reeves. Bass kept an eye on him. Recognized the man as someone he'd arrested before, someone who'd been caught running whiskey. Obvious to the deputy, Hoyt was trying to stay out of his sight, trying his best to avoid eye contact, but all he did was look suspicious. The canvas bags on that mule had an odd appearance, it seemed.

"Willie, hold onto Big Red here. I need to go talk to that feller yonder." Bass indicated Hoyt at the other end of the barge.

"Mornin'," Reeves said, approaching the man from behind. Hoyt jumped a foot. Bass lit up a smoke. Shook the flame from the match and exhaled his drag, flipping the matchstick into the river. Smiling cordially at the man, he said, "I'm Deputy Marshal Reeves. Ain't you J.R. Hoyt?"

J. L. smiled back weakly. "Jay El," he corrected. "Yep."

"Thought so" Bass said. "I never forget a face. Believe I arrested you about two year ago for introducin'. How'd that go for you?

"I paid my fine, done my time," Hoyt answered.

Bass nodded. "Good, good. Man oughta pay his debts. 'Specially his law-breakin' ones." He looked at Hoyt's lumpy saddlebags.

"What you got in them bags?" he asked.

Hoyt moved to get between Reeves' line of sight and his saddlebags. "Aw, ain't nothin'. Just some personal stuff."

"Personal, huh? Mind if I take a look?" Reeves started moving toward the mule.

"No, now hold on, deputy." Put a hand on Reeve's chest. "You got no right to start lookin' in there."

Bass looked down at Hoyt's hand on his vest, then his eyes. He smiled. "Reckon you're right, J. L." Reached down, removed the strap of rawhide off his Colt's hammer, and un-holstered the pistol.

Hoyt's eyes circled big with alarm. He jerked his hand from Bass's chest, stepped back. "Wait a minute, deputy. What're you doin'? I ain't done nothin'!"

Bass chuckled. "Well, if you won't let me check the inside of them bags, I'll just check the outside." He turned the Peacemaker over holding it like a hatchet, smacked the butt-end against a bulge in the bag nearest him. It produced a muffled sound of glass breaking. A wet stain started to spread at the bottom of the bag, a sweet pungent liquid began to drip from the seam. Bass sniffed.

Hoyt looked sick. "Well, damn, Deputy. Why'd you go and do that?"

"That smells a powerful lot like whiskey," Bass said.

Hoyt looked out across the river. "Aw, hell," he said.

"You know I'm going to have to arrest you. Appears you're a backslider on this liquor introducin'."

"It ain't that much," Hoyt pleaded. "I'd be willin' to share it with you."

Reeves undid the straps on the bag. "Don't make it worser, J. L." Removed the pieces of the shattered bottle, tossing them into the river, then took the bags from the mule's rump. "Now come on back with me to the prisoner wagon. I'm gonna have to shackle you."

"What about my mule?"

"We don't shackle mules."

Bill Leach had pulled up to a spot near a clear creek near a stand of cottonwoods shading a bend. "We'll camp here," he said, not seeking anyone else's say. They'd gone on south of old Fort Cobb a couple miles. Now that the Indian fighter Phil Sheridan had moved the military down closer to the Texas border to fight renegades, establishing Fort Sill, the only souls that occupied the land around the abandoned outpost were the Kiowa and Comanche people, along with the few white and black settlers brave enough to live among them. Of course, most of those were outlaws, themselves about as mean and hard as their Indian neighbors, if not more so. That's where the Bruner brothers had settled in.

Hoyt sat on the ground near the prisoner wagon eating his supper. The guardsman, Willie, had chained him to a wheel, Hoyt currently being the only occupant for the wagon. He studied Reeves, who sat at the base of a tree with his warrant book open going over the papers inside, most likely the warrants and writs he'd brung with him, Hoyt decided. The deputy furrowed his brow, his face scowled with confusion and frustration, and he muttered to himself. His plate of food sat beside him untouched, getting colder by the minute.

"What's got you so upset, deputy?" Hoyt asked. Knew Reeves couldn't read.

"These damn writs," Bass answered. "Thought I had them straightened out when we left Fort Smith. Now I ain't so sure."

"You want me to look 'em over for ya?"

Bass looked up, his expression relaxing some. "You can read?" he asked.

"Dang good," Hoyt bragged. "My ma made me stay in school back in Missouri 'til I's eleven. Stepdad finally put a stop to it, though. Said I didn't need to know no readin' or writin' to work hogs."

Bass stood and walked over to Hoyt, handing him three sets of papers. "It's the damn Bruners, tell me which one of these is which."

"I know about them Bruner brothers," Hoyt said. "They's a mean bunch. What they done now?" Hoyt looked over the writs.

"Seminole Lighthorse had 'em locked up for horse theivin', but they busted out, kilt the guard," Bass said. "Then they went and robbed a store in Anadarko, shot and kilt the owner and his ten-year-old boy."

Handing the papers back to Bass one at time, Hoyt said, "This'uns Ransom, this'uns John, this'uns Perro."

Bass grunted, nodding. Thought a minute. "Look here, Hoyt," he said. "Whiles we on this trip, I'd like to take you on as my posseman. I pay you posseman wages. I gonna need yer help with these writs, and I gonna need yer help when we meet up with them Bruners.

"Now, I still got to take you back to Fort Smith and turn you over to the court for introducin'. Ain't no getting' around that, but you do me good, don't run off, I'll speak to Judge Parker about you, testify to what you done to help the law. Mebbe ol' Parker go easy on ya."

"Well . . ." Hoyt scratched the back of his head, considering Reeves' offer. "Hmm, them Bruners, I don't know . . . you gonna unshackle me then? Give me back my gun and mule?"

"Yep, I'll do that. You do me wrong, though, I'll shoot you myself."

Hoyt laughed. "Reckon, that there's a offer I can't turn down."

Bass turned to his guardsman. "Willie, unhitch the prisoner."

"Old Tecumsey live over hill dare, past creek. Mebbe two mile," Willie said pointing to the rise on the horizon. They'd gotten information the Bruners would be holed up either at their pa's, or their older brother Perro's place. Reeves wanted to look at Tecumseh's place first.

"Bill, you and Willie set up camp here. Hoyt, you come with me," Bass said. Spurred Big Red forward.

J. L., sitting a-saddle his mule, watched horse and rider trot off down the trail. "Damn," he said. Agreeing to sign on didn't figure this. Might be better to face a year in the Fort Smith jail than the Bruner brothers. "There's three of them, agin the two of us," he hollered to Reeves. "Four if you count the old man."

Almost everyone in this part of the Territory knew about the Bruners. Mixed blood Shawnee and Negro, the descriptions—mean, ruthless, and cold-blooded—not adequate to describe them. Their daddy, Tecumseh, the product of a French trapper and a Shawnee woman; the boys' ma, an African slave Tecumseh had acquired after she'd come to the tribe following a raid against some Cherokee. Their daddy had brought the boys up rough, all of them meaner'n fifty red hogs. They'd killed and robbed several times before, but because they'd all been concerning Indians, no law outside the tribal police much cared about them. Now that they'd killed a white man and his boy, white man's law decided to pay attention and come after them. Even with Bass Reeves out to bring them in, odds didn't look good they'd succeed, especially west of the Dead Line.

The cabin sat out in the open surrounded on three sides by a six-acre cornfield not more than thirty yards from it. They rode toward the shack at a trot. When they got within two hundred yards, two men came out onto the porch and watched them for several seconds, broke at a run for the cornfield. One carried a rifle, the other had two six guns strapped to his hips.

"Wonder what that was all about?" Hoyt asked.

"Believe those might be a couple of our boys," Bass answered. "We'll ride on up to the house just like they ain't nothin' wrong. I'll go in and talk to the old man, see if them was two of his boys."

"Well, if it were two of them damn Bruners, they might sit out in that corn and pick us off. Sorta makes me nervous. Now see here, deputy, I ain't got no damn quarrel with these boys."

"Jist take it easy, Hoyt. I give you back your mule, I give you back your gun. That's why I'm payin' you posseman wages."

"Well, I shore ain't seen none of it, yet. No sir, I don't like this a damn bit."

"You jist sit tight, and let me do the talkin'."

They dismounted at the front of the cabin, keeping their horses between themselves and the cornfield. Bass understood Hoyt's concern, didn't disagree with it, neither. Knew it'd be suicide to go out wandering in that cornfield looking for them boys. Could be they was smarter than he thought.

He slid the rawhide loop off the Colt's hammer, turned to the cabin door. "Anyone inside?" he yelled.

An old man appeared in the doorway. Wore a pointed crown flat-brim hat, thick braids of salt and pepper hair fell well down across his stooped shoulders onto his thin chest. His brown Paleolithic face was as craggy and weathered as the old hills of the Wichitas.

"Tecumsey Bruner?" Bass called out to him.

The elder nodded.

"I'm Deputy Marshal Reeves." He got no acknowledgement from the man on the porch. "Was them boys who ran out of here your sons?" he asked.

Tecumseh Bruner waited a few seconds. "One of them; one was Frank Buck," he answered.

"Which one of your boys was it?"

"The taller one. He is John."

"Where are your other two, Perro and Ransom?"

Tecumseh shrugged. "Perhaps they are at Perro's place. I have not seen them today."

"Well, why'd them boys run off?" Bass asked.

"John saw you riding up. Said he knew you. Was thinkin' you were coming with papers to arrest them."

Bass shook his head and laughed, looking out at the cornfield. “Naw, I’m out here lookin’ for a horse thief and whiskey runner named George Mack. Your boys knowin’ this country, thought they might could help me out.” He paused looking up at the old Indian, waiting for him to respond. “I don’t even know that other fella. What’s his name again?”

Another pause from Tecumseh. “Frank Buck,” he said.

“Well, Mister Bruner, why don’t you go out to that cornfield and tell them boys to come on back. I’d sure like to find this Mack feller.”

The old man looked unsure. Turned his nervous gaze to the cornfield. “Why don’t you go?” he asked.

Bass shook his head and smiled. “Just don’t want to cause no confusion,” he said. “I went in there lookin’ for ’em,” he motioned toward the cornfield with his head. “They might shoot out of nervousness, especially if’n they think I’s tryin’ to arrest ‘em, like you say.”

He turned back to his horse and adjusted some saddle latigo. “You go tell ’em I ain’t got no paper on ’em, jist want to talk about George Mack. Tell ’em, they help me, I’ll make it worth they time.”

The old Indian sidled toward the cornfield. Bass and Hoyt waited some twenty minutes before the elder returned. He went to a lone rocker on the porch to sit, starting a slow swing. Bass waited for him to speak.

“They would not come out,” Tecumseh said. “John said he would meet you daybreak tomorrow at forks of the road.”

Bass and Hoyt looked at each other. “Him and that Buck feller?” the deputy asked.

The old man nodded. "They will bring Perro and Ransom, too."

"Is that right," Bass said. He gave out a mirthless snort. "Well, where's this fork in the road at?"

Tecumseh motioned with his hand. "Follow the road north, you will find it."

Bass reined Big Red around, and headed back toward their camp; Hoyt followed. They'd ridden a mile before Hoyt spoke. "You really gonna meet them boys tomorrah, deputy? Out there on that road?"

"Reckon so," Bass said.

"Why'd you lie to 'em 'bout havin' papers? They gotta know you's come out here to arrest them."

"Maybe they does, maybe they don't. Need to plant a little uncertainty in they heads."

"Yeah," Hoyt scratched the back of his neck. "But it jist don't seem right, a lawman lyin' to uh outlaw."

A small smirk came to Reeves's lips. "Ain't much honor dealin' with outlaws, 'specially killers. I does whatever it take to make my arrests. The 'portant thing is, y'understand, is that them boys think we ain't gonna draw on 'em. Now tomorrah, we meet up with 'em, we have a little talk, make 'em think I's gonna pay 'em some to help find this other outlaw, and when they's all relaxed and off-guard, we'll throw down on 'em and arrest 'em."

They rode on some in silence. Hoyt shook his head and said, "Damn."

Day had not broken when they got there, to that forks in the road. The trees still held a dimness, the sky had turned a gun barrel gray. The sun hadn't appeared yet. Bass wanted it that way, wanted to arrive in the shadows ahead of the sun and ahead of the Bruners. He wanted to hear them ride in, know where they were. He wanted to meet them at his stand, not the other way around. Reeves and Hoyt dismounted, waited in the trees.

"You know this Buck fella?" Bass asked.

"Seen him oncest in Anadarko," Hoyt answered. "He come into this store I's at . . . place I used to do bidness with, you know, back in my, um, tradin' days. Anyways . . . this Buck feller pushed his way to the bar past a Mexican vaquero who didn't much like bein' shoved. The vaquero pulled a knife on Buck, who drew and shot that boy faster'n you could spit. They's other talk of him; fancies himself a gunslinger. Wears two white bone-handled guns with the butts pointed out. Ain't heard when he took up and started ridin' with them Bruners."

Reeves thought on that information for a while. "Them boys get here, I'll try to distract 'em with talk about helpin' me find George Mack. When they's all relaxed, ain't payin' attention, I'll throw down on 'em, tell 'em they's under arrest. You need to be ready, draw on 'em, too. Need to get the drop on 'em afore they can do anything about it."

"Don't believe I can outdraw Frank Buck," Hoyt said.

"I'll take care of Buck, you just take care of them Bruners," Bass said.

"All three of 'em?"

"Stand over by your mule when they ride up, then you can get behind him when we draw down. That way if one likely draws and shoots, he'll hit your mule first, and you can fire back."

"Reckon I can do that, but I'd hate for ol' Buster to take a bullet."

"Up to you," Bass said with a shrug. "Just thought it'd be better him than you."

The top rim of the sun just started to nudge above the eastern hills when they heard the riders coming. "Don't sound like four horses," Bass said.

Reeves looked around the post oak he stood behind to see two riders coming down the left fork. With the rising sun on the riders' faces, he could see it was John Bruner and the man Buck.

"Don't look like you'll have three Bruners to worry about," Bass said to Hoyt. "Stay here in the trees and pay attention. We'll still need to get the drop on these two."

He stepped out from the trees.

The riders reined up twenty feet away. "Mornin' deputy," Bruner said.

"Your pappy said you's comin' with your brothers," Bass answered.

Bruner leaned his forearms onto the saddle horn. "They had some chores to attend. Said they'd meet us back at Perro's place."

Bass nodded, looked back up the left fork behind the two men, then out to the right fork and the woods between them. "Well, I'm out lookin' for a man named George Mack. You know where I can find him?"

"We can help you ketch him, you make it worth our time, me and Frank here."

"We bring him in, I'll pay you two dollars apiece."

Bruner nodded, looking at his partner, back at Reeves. "How I know you ain't got papers on me, wantin' to take me in?"

Bass gave Bruner a wry smile, eyed Buck. "Why'd you think that, John? They a reason I should have paper on ya? Or your friend here?"

Bruner fidgeted, gave out a nervous laugh, and looked around. Frank Buck kept his cold stare on Reeves, his right hand resting on his thigh, knuckles and thumb down. "Where's your partner I seen you with yesterday?" Bruner asked.

Hoyt walked out from the trees leading his mule. "Haddy," he said.

"You boys get on down, let's set," Bass said. "I'll get my book out and we'll talk about where to find this Mack fella." Walked over to Big Red and untied his rain slicker rolled up behind the cantle, removed his warrant book from the saddlebag.

"We can set on this slicker t'keep the dew off'n us." Bass tucked the book under one arm, spread the slicker out on the ground, and sat cross-legged at one corner. The two outlaws looked at him curiously. Bass looked up at them. "Well, c'mon, boys. Take a load off."

The two men dismounted, each taking a corner of the slicker. Hoyt stayed next to Buster, slightly behind him. Bruner looked at him. "You standin' behind that mule makes me kinda nervous, mister. Ain't y'neighborly?"

Bass motioned Hoyt over. He advanced reluctantly, squatting between the deputy and Buck. Bass went to searching through his warrant book. "Got that writ for Mack in here somewheres," he said. "Man's wanted for stealin' some horses out around Tishamingo, also for shootin' a Lighthorse, I believe." He continued to sort the tri-folded documents, opening and looking at each one as he came to it, jabbering on about this and that hoping the dullness of it would distract the outlaws.

Buck yawned, turned to look up the left fork. Bruner started to get impatient. "Why you wantin' to show me papers on George Mack? I don't care nothin' about that. Let's just get on down the road." He looked over his shoulder.

"Well, it's important you know it's legal, who we goin' after, if'n you's to be my possemen," Bass said. He unfolded one more document.

"Ah, here it is," he said, folding it back and handing it to Bruner with his left hand, who snatched it angrily with his right hand.

"Why you handing this to me?" Bruner said, clearly irritated. "Hell, deputy, I can't read it anyways."

Reeves, with the speed of a striking rattler, drew out his Peacemaker and cocked back the hammer, pointing it between Bruner's eyes. "That there one's for you, John. I'm placing you under arrest for murder."

"Why you lyin' bastard," Bruner said. He slapped the warrant down onto the slicker. "You told me you didn't have no papers on me."

"Don't believe I did, John. It was your daddy I lied to."

Buck reached with his left to his right pistol, starting to stand. Hoyt lunged, grabbing Buck's wrist before he could extract the bone-handled gun all the way. Fumbled to draw out his own pistol, but not before Buck yanked his arm free from Hoyt's grip, backing away.

"You put yer gotdamn hands up," Hoyt commanded. He stood, too, and stumbled forward; cocked his Colt and aimed it at Buck's chest.

"Hell, I give up, I give up!" Buck said, raising his right hand, still backing. Reached for his right gun with his left hand, turning sideways to the posseman.

"Shoot him!" Bass yelled. Hoyt fired, the round went wide.

"Goddamit! I give up!" Buck yelled, twisted more to his right throwing his left arm up; reached with his right for the left gun. Hoyt cocked and fired a second time, the bullet nicking the bottom of Buck's left forearm. The outlaw swore and turned back to his left, reaching for the right gun. Swung it out, bringing it to bear on Hoyt when the deputy's big Colt blasted. The slug hit Buck square in the chest, he kicked backward falling hard to the ground, the pistol flying from his hand. One leg twitched twice, and he lay still.

Bruner stood pulling out his own gun when Bass had swung to fire on Buck, but the deputy caught Bruner's movement out of the corner of his eye. He grabbed the barrel of Bruner's pistol, pushing it away from his head just as the outlaw pulled the trigger. The hot barrel seared his palm, but he didn't let go, brought his own pistol down hard across Bruner's left ear knocking him cold.

Hoyt stood shaking and breathing hard. "Damn, deputy, Damn," he said.

"You ain't much of a shot," Bass said.

"Hell, I never claimed to be. Had no idee you'd put me to shootin'. 'Sides, you said you's goin' to take care of Buck. Damn."

A .45 slug splintered a chunk out of the post oak behind Bass's head, another seared Hoyt's neck just below his jawbone, the reports of two distant rifle shots came a fraction of a second behind them.

Hoyt hollered and grabbed his neck, Buster and Big Red bolted, and Bass crouched, duck-walking to get behind the oak. "Damn, I'm hit!" Hoyt yelled, still standing there looking around.

"Get down!" Bass yelled.

The posseman came to his senses and obeyed, just as two more bullets twanged off trees, their reports echoed from the left fork.

"How bad ya hit?" Bass asked.

A few seconds passed before Hoyt answered. "Bullet creased my neck. Bleedin' like a stuck hog, and it hurts like hell. I don't reckon they kilt me, though."

"Must be them other two Bruner boys," Bass said. "Guess they figured to bushwhack us down the road, couldn't wait oncest they seen us take down John and Buck."

Two more shots ricocheted through the trees.

"I see where they's firing from," Bass said. "Out of range for these pistols. I can cut around through these woods and get behind 'em. You keep firing to keep 'em busy. Move around some, so's they'll think it still the two of us here."

Reeves crabbed backwards into the trees and undergrowth. When he far enough, rose to a crouch and moved to his left, paralleling the road. Their attackers continued to fire, and Hoyt answered every so often.

One of the gunmen had positioned himself on the far side of the road just out of the trees; the other had set up behind a limestone slab jutting out of the ground with two red cedars flanking it. When Bass got to a point slightly behind the two gunmen, he remained squatting in the trees, looking over the situation, thinking it out.

The man at the limestone outcrop was about twenty yards behind the other across the road; his attention, and the other man's, fully on Hoyt's location. Bass thought he could come up behind the man at the rock and take him down—most likely he could do it without the other man across the road taking notice. Weren't so sure about how to handle that guy. He wanted to take all these Bruners alive, but he'd do what he had to do even if that meant shooting one of them.

Ransom Bruner never knew what hit him. All he'd remember later, when he started to come around, one second he'd been sighting down the barrel of his Henry repeater, aiming at the top of a man's head, the next, blackness. Didn't even feel any pain at the time, although the achy knot above and to the back of his right ear, gave throbbing testimony to the cold steel whack of the .44 gun barrel. Confusion swam through his foggy mind as to why he lay across his saddle watching the ground go by beneath him. Why his feet were bound together, his hands tied to a rope that went under the horses belly and to his ankles.

"Perro?" he wailed with a hoarse voice. But his older brother didn't answer.

Another voice, a deep bass in front of him, said, "Your brother can't talk right now."

Things started to come back to Ransom. They'd been waiting to ambush Deputy Bass Reeves and his posseman; John was gonna bring 'em up the road past where they were waiting. But something had gone wrong, and he and Perro had started shooting.

"What did you do to Perro?" Ransom asked.

"I shot him," the voice answered.

"Who's that talkin'?" Ransom asked.

"Deputy Marshal Bass Reeves."

"You kilt my brothers?" Ransom's voice had an angry whine.

"John ain't dead," Reeves answered. "He just ain't come to yet, like you. Tied to the horse behind you.

"Perro, now," Bass continued. "I shot him twice when he refused to put down his rifle after I told him to. Fired on me, so I shot him in the thigh, that didn't stop him neither. So I creased his skull with a bullet. Figure it jist bounced off, it bein' too hard for a .44 slug to pass through. Ain't dead yet, but he's bleedin' pretty good, and it's a long way back to Fort Smith."

There was a fourth horse with a body draped over it, one wrapped in a canvas slicker, that of Frank Buck.

Reeves said to his posseman, who rode next to him, "You done okay today, Hoyt. Not only goin' to pay you double wages for your trouble, but not going to bring up to Judge Parker about your lastest whiskey sellin'. Figure we can let that go for now, 'sides, I destroyed all the evidence. Do need to ax you one more favor, though."

"Thad be whut?" Hoyt asked.

"We get back to Fort Smith, I need you to say you's the one shot Frank Buck."

"Why hell, Bass, you shot him fair 'n square. Most likely saved my life. Ever thing you done out here with them Bruners were just about the bravest thing I ever seen."

Reeves shifted some in the saddle, scratched an armpit. "Jist the same," he said. "I'd sure 'preciate it if you done that."

Hoyt looked at Reeves, studying his face, trying to read what the man was thinking. Figured he knew. Newspapers didn't always get their stories straight. Most times as not, whoever wrote things up told 'em the way they wanted to, according to how they felt. Didn't appear true facts was all that important in newspapers. Were more about what they thought folks who read the stories wanted to hear . . . or didn't want to hear. One of the things folks didn't want to hear was that a colored deputy shot and killed a white man, even one as no 'count as the killer Frank Buck. To Hoyt's way of thinkin' Deputy Marshal Bass Reeves was ten times the man of any scribblin' snivelin' newspaper man. Wondered why such small men had such a big power.

"Aw right," Hoyt said. "If'n that's what you want, I'll do that for you, deputy."

# Dupery at Corncob Forks

*Bass didn't allus have t'shoot hisself out of ever sit'chashun. They was times he used his own wit to bring in outlaws. Truth be knowed, I believe he much preferred it that way. Now, don't get me wrong. Bass was good with a gun and rifle as anyone, better'n most; but he was a sharp-minded man, too. I believe his wits done more to keep him alive than any firearm. Still, bein' as how he were a Baptist deacon, he chose not to shoot no one, if'n he could help it. So what he'd do sometimes is put on disguises and pretend he was someone he weren't so's he could get in amongst them outlaws to make arrests afore they figgered out what was goin' on. Course, they's partic'lar outlaws had about half the wits Bass did, so his dupery, as he called it, worked better on some than others. – Posseman Jud Coldstone*

Bursting through the door, Dooley Cuder shouted, "Pull yer pants up!"

Wanted to sound clever and meant to say, "Pull yer hands out yer pants and git 'em up!" but in his excitement it didn't come out that way.

He and his brother Truman had ridden their mule up to Honest Pete's Trading Post near the settlement of Purdy, and figured it to be as good a place as any to rob. Truman allowed as how they could likely get in and out of there without much trouble, it being on the edge of town with no real law around.

Pete Hopper, the proprietor of the trading post, had founded the town, and was the closest thing it had to a marshal. The tale was, the day Pete and his now dead wife had rolled up to the singing creek overspread by tall cottonwoods, their tops rustling in the soft breeze, and the rolling grassy hills sparkling with dew on that cool June morning almost two decades past, the missus had sighed and said, "This here is right purdy," so that's what Pete named the spot and, eventually, the small town that sprung up around his establishment.

Cuder boys knew Pete; had done business with him trading hogs for goods. They thought (not one of the boys' strengths) it'd be better to rob someone they knew, than not. So there they stood just inside the door with neckerchiefs pulled over their noses; Dooley pointing a double barreled ten-gauge Greener, Truman his ancient Colt Dragoon.

The only people in the store at the time were Pete, a trapper they called Long John Pierre, and his Kickapoo wife everyone knew as Catfish Sally. Pierre and Pete stood at the back counter having a discussion about the pelts Pierre had brought in, and Catfish Sally was by the knife case at the south wall looking over a bone-handled Bowie.

Long John and Pete looked up at the two intruders somewhat puzzled. Looked like a hold up, but after Dooley's command they weren't right sure. "Do what?" Pete asked.

"He meant 'reach for the sky, this here's a hold-up.' Let's git on with it." Truman said. He hooked a boot out and kicked Dooley in the seat of his pants, snarling, "You idjit."

"Yeah, put yer pants on!" Dooley said. He'd started dancing around like an agitated circus bear.

Pierre and Pete traded looks. The trapper looked at the floor and shook his head. Catfish Sally, who had opened the glass knife case to take out the Bowie for a better look, put it back and closed the glassed lid. Truman watched her, looked back at the two men at the counter.

"We ain't foolin' here," Truman said. To emphasize his point, he eared back the Dragoon's hammer.

"Truman, why you and Dooley wearing them damn bandanas over yer noses?" Pete asked. "I know who you are. Hell, when ya come in, that pig smell alone give ya away."

The two brothers glanced at one another. Truman raised his pistol and fired it into the log rafters, the boom of the hand cannon deafening in the close confines. Dooley whooped and danced. Truman cocked the revolver again and pointed it at Pete. "That don't matter," he said. "Just put yer hands up and gimme all yer money."

"And two boxes of them 10 gauges," Dooley added, hopping around in a two foot circle.

Pierre and Sally complied with their hands as did the store owner. "Aw right," Pete said with a sigh. "Ain't no need to get all riled." He eyed Dooley with real concern. "You watch yerself with that Greener, Dooley." To which the latter gave out another whoop and danced some more.

Pete looked back at the eldest Cuder brother. "I don't think you thought this all the way through, Truman."

The robber's eyes narrowed with suspicion. "Whadda you mean?"

"How am I going to get you my money with my hands up?"

Truman furrowed his brow and pondered a few seconds. "Dooley, you get over there and get Pete's money out t'drawer." Waving his pistol barrel, he added, "Pete, you and Pierre go stand over there by Sally. And keep yer hands up!"

Dooley went behind the counter, looking under it. Pulled out the cash box and a Colt Peacemaker. "Why looka here," he said. Still holding the pistol, he pointed it toward Pete, skipped back and forth. "You damn ol' baster, you's aimin' to pull out this pistol on us, wasn't ya?"

"Jist shut up and open the cash box," Truman said.

Dooley shoved the pistol into his pants waist and opened the cash box. "They damn sure ain't much in here," he said with disgust.

Truman went over to see for himself, keeping the trio of hostages covered. Looked in the open box. "This all you got, Hopper?"

"Yep," Pete answered. "This here's a tradin' post. We don't deal much in cash money."

Truman looked around trying to see what he could take that wouldn't burden them down too much. Dooley did the same, looking under the counter again. He pulled out a gray canvas bag that had some heft, dropping it onto the countertop with a thunk. "What the hell is this?" he asked.

"Boys," Honest Pete said with a certain gravity in his voice. "If'n you take my money and whatever else you want in this post, then all's you got to deal with is me. You take what's in that canvas bag, you're gonna be in a whole lot bigger trouble. They'll send marshals out for ya. That there is the United States mail. They don't take kindly to it bein' stole."

Truman reached over and picked up the bag testing its weight. "Is they any money in it?"

"Doubt it," Pete answered. "Mostly letters to folks around here. Might be some stuff goes out to Fort Sill, official military binness. Don't believe you'd want to take that." Pete figured if these stupid Cuder boys took that mail, he could let the Federal law deal with them; it'd save him the trouble and expense.

"Well, we'll just have a look-see," Truman said, grabbing up the bag and putting it under his left arm.

Dooley had turned to look on the shelves behind him scanning the boxes of ammunition. "Which one of these is ten-gauges?" he asked. Like Truman, he couldn't read.

"Top shelf, on your right," Pete said.

Dooley grabbed a couple boxes. "These un's?"

"Nope, yer other right."

Truman walked over to the group. Looked down into the knife case. "You like that big knife, do ya, Sally?"

The young Indian woman nodded.

Truman shattered the top glass of the case with his pistol barrel.

"Got dammit, Truman!" Pete said. "Why'd you go and do that? All you had to do was open the lid."

Truman looked at Pete, reached in for the Bowie and handed it to Sally. "I'm stealin' this and givin' it to you, Sally. I think you oughta have it."

Sally looked at Truman for a few seconds, took the offered knife.

"Let's go, Dooley," Truman said to his brother, and the two started backing out of the trading post.

At the door Truman stopped. "You best not follow us," he said to Pete, and fired the Dragoon into the rafters again to emphasize his point. The group cringed at the noise;

Truman noticed Pete looked more pissed than scared. "We ain't gonna follow ya, Truman," Pete said. "You headed home?"

Truman shrugged. "Most likely," he said. Realizing his mistake, he amended, "No, we's prolly gonna go summers else." He looked at the men to see if either had bought it. When Pete nodded, turned, ran out the door, and jumped onto the back of the mule behind Dooley. Dooley kicked the mule's flanks, and it trotted down the road towards home.

The trio in the store watched as the two bandits rode off, bouncing along on the mule's back. Sally handed the Bowie back to Pete.

Normally, Pete would let something like this go. Had no intention of following them. Hell, he knew where they lived. The Cuder boys were uncommonly stupid, but he knew their ma, and depended on them to bring him good hogs. He figured they was just restless or drunk, maybe both. He could've just deducted the boxes of shotgun shells and the damages to his knife case from the price he'd pay the next time they came to trade their pigs, and, of course, get his pistol back. But now that they'd stolen that mail sack, he'd have to report them to the Federal law in Arkansas.

By the time the court in Fort Smith had issued the writ for the Cuder brothers' arrest for the mail theft at Purdy, I.T., the boys had committed two more felonies. One was an armed robbery of a train depot, from which they made away with twenty-five dollars and the depot man's pocket watch. Truman had also shot the clerk in the leg—with Pete

Hopper's Peacemaker—when the man tried to make a break for the door. The other crime was an attempted mule theft.

Concerning the latter, they'd reasoned they needed a second mule, and coming upon a man plowing, decided to take his. Unfortunately, Dooley, during the nervous dance he always did when robbing, accidently discharged the Greener hitting the harnessed mule in the neck, killing it instantly. Some of the shot struck the farmer in the wrist and hand that held the throat latch strap at the mule's head. So not only did the Cuder brothers have the charge of theft of the U.S. mail hung on them, but also two felony charges for assaults with a firearm, and one for destruction of private property.

As it happened, the mail bag the Cuder brothers stole had in it a small box of gold coins—five twenty dollar double eagles—meant for the provost at Fort Sill to use as reward money. These were due two scouts who'd aided in rounding up a renegade Comanche named Bleeding Dog and his band who'd been terrorizing farmers in North Texas. Normally, the government didn't send cash money through the U.S. Mail, especially gold coins, but an underling bureaucrat back in Washington had screwed up. However, one man's screw up can be another man's reward; in this case in the form of $1,000 each on the heads of the outlaws Truman and Dooley Cuder.

As the Federal government operates in such things, regulations stated a fixed amount to post as a reward for Federal law-breakers, be they assassins or mail robbers. Nobody within the insular bubble of government, elected to office or appointed to the Civil Service, questioned the offering of a $2,000 reward for the arrest of two one-hundred-dollar moron thieves.

The Court commissioner informed Deputy Bass Reeves two more writs were forthcoming on the Cuder brothers, but there was that $2,000 reward, so Reeves wanted to leave out as soon as possible before anyone else got to them. Word travelled fast throughout the bounty rich I.T. One writ, that for stealing mail, would be enough to bring the Cuders in, Bass reasoned; all the rest would be gravy.

Deputy Reeves had a full book, so took along in his outfit the usual complement of personnel: one posseman, one guard and prisoner wagon, one cook and his wagon.

In the damp early morning of their third day, they pulled out from camp near the Seminole settlement of Konawa. A heavy spray saturated the air making it hard to tell where the fog left off and the mist began. Not much could be seen beyond thirty feet, the cold wet November air was deathly still.

Bill the cook sat the bench of the grub wagon in his usual foul mood. Guardsman Willie Jumps a Creek, suffering from a bout of the grippe, lagged the prisoner wagon far behind the others due to his frequent stops to run into the woods. Those stops dampened the disposition of the prisoners more than the bone-chilling mist.

"Gol-dangit, Willie," the one-armed prisoner Lefty Shoemaker groused. "You keep goin' off and leaving us out here alone, some renegade Comanch is liable to come along, take our boots and steal our hair." He'd lost his right arm at Wilson's Creek back in '61, had taken up whiskey selling to the Indians as a trade, which landed him in the prisoner wagon again.

"Why don't you shut the hell up, Shoemaker? I'm tryin' to get some sleep here," said the horse thief Mannford Sizemore.

"RRRAANPH! Both uh yourn!" growled the one they called Buffalo Jake. Called him that mainly because he looked and smelled like one, a plains bison, wearing a wooly buffalo hide over most of his massive body, had so much hair and beard one could barely see his nose and eyes; his mouth, neck and ears having to be assumed. Was rumored he'd once crushed a man's head with his bare hands. Buffalo Jake was being hauled in for disemboweling a tinhorn gambler in a dispute over a dealt hand of cards. Knowing those things, Lefty and Sizemore took heed of Jake's request to keep quiet.

Up ahead, Deputy Reeves and his posseman, Jud Coldstone, let their horses walk along picking their way semi-blindly through the soup.

"How you figger on us gettin' them Cuder boys, Bass?" Jud asked the question as much to make conversation as to find out the deputy's plans.

"Been thinkin' on that, Jud," Bass said. "As stupid and gun happy as them boys seem to be, I reckon the best way to get to 'em is by dupery."

"By do-whut?"

"Dupery. That means foolin' 'em."

"How we gonna do that?"

"Well, first off, they ain't gone be no *we*. I figger on goin' in there alone, makin' out like I'm some kind of outlaw like them, gettin' 'em to trust me, then cuffin' 'em up and arrested when they ain't expectin' it."

"Whadda ya want me to do?"

"Stay at camp and keep Bill the Cook and Buffalo Jake from killin' anyone."

Bass always brought along a wardrobe for his pretenses, his favorite to give him the look of a poor, itinerant black man who didn't appear to be a threat. Consisted of an old pair of ragged overalls, some worn out shoes he'd knocked the heels off of, and a sweat-stained old floppy felt hat he'd shot three holes through. Carried a bandana poke with some other essentials in it, among them his Colt and two pair of handcuffs. They'd pulled up to make camp a good distance from Purdy, maybe twelve, fourteen miles. Bass said he wanted to walk to the Cuder place from where they'd set up camp so he'd look like the road tramp he wanted them to think he was.

Already knew where the Cuder boys lived as Mister Hopper had informed the court of their whereabouts when he'd telegraphed the complaint. They had a shack and some hog pens that sat in the vee of a forked road with a big cornfield behind it. Folks knew the location as Corncob Forks. The Cuders had grown pigs and corn there for twenty years. Sam Cuder built the place, but died of a copperhead bite ten years back; the missus and two boys had taken care of things since.

Bass walked upon the place looking the part he'd wanted—dusty, thirsty, cold, hungry, and tired. His feet hurt, the worn-out old heelless shoes had worn blisters from the fifteen mile walk. As he approached, a large woman in a dirty cotton dress came out onto the porch and watched him. A head of gray-streaked black hair pulled up in a loose bun sat above her broad face. She had a single thick brow across wide-set eyes, a flat nose and thick lips. A big black mole popped out below her lower lip with a tuft of hair growing out of it like clump of briars. Set her mouth in a snarl; yellowish-black and jagged teeth added to the menace. Pointed a Greener at Bass.

"Whut t'hell do you want?" she asked the tramp.

Bass removed his hat, looked apologetic. "Evenin', ma'am. I's jist passin' through. I's, uh, well, the law's after me, and I's tryin' to lose 'em in these here woods. I's jist wonderin' if'n I could get a drink of water from yo' well over yonder."

"Whut the law want you fer?"

Bass chuckled and tried to look even more sorry. Bowed his head , shook it side-to-side, keeping his eyes mostly on the ground. "Well, they's a passel things, but today it's 'cause I stole me some money from a sto'. I got in and stole they money, got plum away afo' they even knowed it. Got me a good head start, but now they's after me. Believe I throwed 'em off'n my trail, though. Ain't seen hide nor hair of 'em fo' two day now."

The woman lowered the Greener some, but kept it in her arms. "Well, I reckon you can have a drink from the well."

"Thank ya, kindly, ma'am. I just go on over there and get me some, then." Bass gestured toward the well and started walking toward it. The woman came down off the porch, followed at a safe distance. Kept the Greener pointed at the ground behind Bass.

"So you's a outlaw," the woman said, more as an assessment than a question.

"Yaz'm, I 'spect you could say that," Bass set his poke on the ground, pulled the bucket up, took the tin dipper off a hook, and brought a dip of water up out of the bucket. Took a long drink, and wiped his mouth with a sleeve. "I ain't a bad outlaw, y'understand; ain't never kilt nobody or nothin'. But I has done me some robbin'. Ain't got a lot from it, but I gets along."

The woman snorted like one of her hogs. "I got me two boys like that. Had 'em out here workin' these hogs 'til my old man got snake bit and died. Idjits got this wild hair and thought they'd go int' outlawin'. Ain't done much good at it, though. Boys's stupid more'n anything else . . . like they pa."

"Well, now, robbin' is sho' nuf sumpin takes some practice t'get good at. My first few times I ain't done so good. Now days, I reckon I brings in fo', fie hunnert a week."

The woman scrunched up her face in a look of doubt, sneering derisively. "I'd say that's hog shit. You don't look like no man what brings in five hunnert a week."

Bass slapped his knee and laughed, weaving up and back like he was going to fall over. "I knows, I knows, an' I's glad you say that. Means I's doin' right. Erryone 'spects me t'look like a po' tramp nigguh, so thas what I gives 'em. That way I's kinda invisible. If'n I go 'round all fancied up and spendin' that money, folks notice me right off, an' starts thinkin' I ain't come by that money honest. It's just a fact, a colored man spendin' money look suspicious."

The woman nodded, looking thoughtful. "Makes damn good sense," she said. "Believe my boys could use some good sense as that."

"Well, now," Bass said. He took another dipperful, removed his hat, and poured the water on his head. He bent over and shook the excess off his head, wiped his face with his sleeves. "I be happy t'help them boys with some advice, mebbe fo' some supper."

The woman lifted the shotgun to her shoulder. With a short laugh, she said, "Hell, you's welcome to try, mister, but I ain't so sure it'd take with them boys. Like I say, they ain't very smart. You's welcome to stay and eat with us, though."

Bass sat on the porch in a chair made of hickory branches, nailed and loosely bound. It had been put together with a few lengths of hemp rope woven to make a seat then run through holes in the frame and knotted. It was far from comfortable, and Bass wasn't sure it'd hold up long to his weight, but it put him in a place to see down the road. Only other choice was to stand, which he was too tuckered to do. Of course, he could sit on the porch boards with his back against the shack wall, but he wanted to be in plain view when the brothers rode up.

When he asked Ma Cuder where the boys were, she said she didn't know for sure, probably out on one of their outlawin' trips, more'n likely they'd be along directly as they always showed up for supper. Bass had his poke with him, in his lap. His Colt was still in there, he arranged it to pull out quickly if need be.

Dooley was the first to spot Reeves. They'd ridden in on the west fork, rounding the intersection and coming into the yard near the hog shed. Dooley pulled up and drew out the dragoon. "Whut t'hell?" he said.

Truman picked up the stranger sitting on their porch, too, yanked out Pete Hopper's Colt from his belt. Since that robbery, Truman had taken ownership of the Peacemaker, and passed the dragoon on to his little brother. Dooley protested, but Truman explained that he was the oldest, therefore, should carry the better weapon. He also thought it'd be safer, after the mule shooting incident, if Dooley carried a pistol rather than the Greener. Dooley didn't like it one damn bit, but he complied under promise of a butt-whipping if he didn't. He'd been the recipient of those since age two and respected the threat.

Truman eared the Peacemaker and pointed it at Reeves. "Whut t'hell you doin' on our porch?"

"Where's ma?" Dooley followed.

"Evenin' boys," Bass said. He smiled and spoke in a cordial, calm voice.

"Git yer hand away from that poke or I'll blast ya." Truman warned.

Bass raised his hands. "Now, take it easy, son. Ain't no call to get all riled up. Yo' ma's awright. She inside cookin' yo' supper. She tole me I could sit out here."

The Cuders looked at one another, then back at Bass. "I'm gonna shoot him anyway," Dooley said. "He's lookin' 'spishus to me. What if'n he's the law?"

Truman considered the man on his porch. "Naw, I don't think he's no law."

"How'd you know?" Dooley responded with scorn in his voice.

"Wull, lookit him. He's colored."

"So what?"

"You idjit. Ain't no law gonna put a badge on a colored man. 'Sides, he ain't wearin' one that I can see."

Dooley deliberated. “Reckon you’re right.” He raised the dragoon again and pointed it at Reeves. “That only means one thing; colored man roamin’ around by hisself, he’s uh outlaw. He’s probly kilt ma, or worser.”

“You idjits put them guns down afore ya hurt yersef!” Ma Cuder had come through the door and stood at the edge of the porch, hands on her stout hips, her right hand gripping a yard-long, inch-thick hickory stick, one that looked like it’s been well-used.

“Ma, you ain’t dead,” Dooley said. His voice sounded more disappointed than relieved.

“No I ain’t dead, you damn idjit. Now, get them mules took care of and come to supper.”

The brothers turned their mounts toward the stable shed in cowed compliance. They’d managed to get a second mule without shooting it, just barely. They’d come upon the animal beside a creek already saddled, riderless, placidly munching grass, its reins tethered to a tree limb by a stream. Presumably its owner was somewhere along the creek fishing. Dooley had pulled the dragoon with the angered intent to blast the beast after it had reached around and bit him on the butt when he first stuck his foot in the left stirrup. Fortunately for the mule Truman stopped Dooley.

Bass and Ma Cuder watched the boys in silence as they ambled their mules toward the stable. “Boys seem a mite edgy,” Bass said after a bit.

Ma Cuder gave out another one of her hog snorts. “They ain’t got sense God give a possum. Don’t know how they’ve stayed alive as long as they have.”

The brothers stomped through the door and came to the table. Dooley stopped to protest before he sat. “Aw, Ma, we havin’ beans and hogback again? ’At’s all we ever have,” he whined.

“You shet up and set down afore I whack ya,” Ma said. She sat herself, propped the hickory rod at the table’s edge next to her. Bass and the boys sat. Dooley reached to grab a chunk of cornbread.

Ma grabbed up the hickory, reached out and whacked Dooley on the left shoulder. He cringed in pain and dropped the cornbread. “Yow! Damn, Ma,” he whimpered, rubbing his shoulder. “Why’d you do that for?”

“We ain’t prayed grace,” she answered, putting the rod back at its place beside her. Folded her hands in front of her and bowed her head. The boys looked at one another in confusion and wonder.

“Lord,” she started. “We surely thank ya fer these vittles, even though it ’uz me and these idjit boys got ’em here to this table . . . mostly me. But, like I say, thank ya anyway. And while yer at it, Lord, I could sure use yer help with these damn boys. They ain’t never been particular bright, so if you could help ’em along their path, be it farmin’ hogs or outlawin’, I’d surely appreciate it. Amen . . . Oh, and we’re glad to have settin’ at our table Mister . . . um, this here colored stranger. Amen again.”

Dooley reached for the cornbread, Ma took up the rod and whacked him again. He recoiled with tears in his eyes. “Where’s yer manners. Let our guest go first,” Ma admonished.

Bass ladled up some beans from the pot, and took a slice of cornbread. "Ain't nothin' I likes better than beans with hogback and cornbread."

"Prayin' there, I realized we ain't got yer name," she said.

Spooning up a mouthful of beans, Bass said, "Smith, Jonesy Smith."

"That's kinda a peculiar name," Truman said.

Bass chuckled. "'Spect it is. I's oncest owned by a man named Smith who sold me to a man named Jones."

The boys nodded and scooped beans. Ma stared at Bass with squinted eyes.

"What you doin' way out here?" Truman asked.

"He's a outlaw," Ma said.

Truman looked at his ma, back at Bass. Dooley kept eating. "Oh yeah?" Truman said. "Me and Dooley is outlaws, too."

"You don't say," Bass responded.

"I damn sure do say. I'm the one's in charge, 'cause Dooley here's a damn idjit."

"Yer both damn idjits," Ma interjected.

"What kinda outlawin' you boys done?" Bass asked.

"Well, we robbed us a train station, stole one of them mules ya seen. Biggest thing we done, though, was steal some double eagles from the gummint."

"You don't say," Bass said. He tried to look impressed.

"Hell yeah, I say it! Why you keep askin' that?"

Bass shrugged. "It's just an expression."

"Uh whut?" Dooley asked.

"Expression," Bass repeated. "A way of sayin' things."

“Whut is it you done, Mister Jones, outlawin’ I mean?” Truman asked.

“It’s Smith, last name’s Smith, but you boys can call me Jonesy.”

The two Cuders looked at one another and scratched their respective heads.

“Aw right then, Mister Jonesy, what outlawin’ you done?” Truman asked again.

Bass shook his head and giggled. “Just Jonesy, boys. Ain’t no need for no ‘mister.’”

“Idjits,” Ma muttered.

“I robs me mostly sto’s,” Bass continued. “They’s usually got the most money plus I can pick me up some food or clothes I might need, but I catches me some men ever now and again. I looks for me a fella seems to be prosperous, mostly at night comin’ out of some saloon or ho’ house. I follows ’em ’til they in a dark place, then I conks ’em on the haid and takes they wallet. I leaves the women folk alone, though, even the ho’s.”

Dooley puffed up a little. “Me and Truman robbed us a store. Made off with a hunnert dollars in gold,” he said.

“Shut up, you idjit,” Truman scolded. He delivered a swift boot toe to Dooley’s shin.

“Is that a fact?” Bass said with feigned admiration.

“Damn sure is,” Dooley said, rubbing his kicked spot and giving his brother a hateful look.

“Mister Smith claims he can make five hunnert dollars a week robbin’,” Ma Cuder said.

The boys looked at each other. “Hell, that ain’t possible,” Truman spat.

“Damn sure is,” Bass said. “If you do it right.”

"How's that?" Truman asked.

"Well, you got to know what you's goin' to do, put a little thinkin' to it. You can't just ride up to a sto' and rob it; you got to study it fo' a few days, see when folks goes in and comes out, what time they opens, what time they closes. Best to rob a sto' right at closin' time, thas when they ain't nobody in there but the sto' keep, thas when he got the mos' money."

Dooley stared at Reeves with mouth-open wonder. Truman nodded. "I ain't never thought of that," he said.

Dooley nodded with a grin and said, "That's jist uh egs-preshun."

Bass laughed and shook his head. "You boys got a lot to learn 'bout outlawin'. Sto's is good to practice robbin' on, but that ain't where the real money be."

"You talkin' 'bout trains?" Truman asked.

"Huh-uh, trains is too risky," Bass answered. "Man could get hurt jumpin' trains. Nah sir, banks is what you wants to rob."

The brothers looked at one another with uncertainty. "We ain't never been in no bank. Seen a couple, but ain't never been in one. What is it they do in 'em to get money?"

"That's where people takes they money, son. Puts it up in there fo' safe keepin' 'til they needs it. Sto's puts they money up in there, too, along with sawmills and such."

Dooley dug into an ear with the nail of his right forefinger, then picked a bean husk from an incisor with same nail. "You ever robbed a bank?"

"Couple, when I's ridin' with some boys. See, that's the thing. Man shouldn't rob a bank by hisself. Needs three, at least."

"How come?" Truman asked.

"Too many people to watch after: folks in there t'puts they money in or takes it out, couple fellas in a cage handin' it out, one or two men sittin' at desks, and usually they's a guard by the doe' with a shotgun."

The conversation went on like that through supper, on into the evening hours. More he talked about his outlawin' expertise, the more impressed the Cuder boys became with Jonesy Smith. Ma Cuder wasn't so sure.

"They's jist sumpin I ain't figgered out, Mister Smith. Despite all you's sayin' about wantin' to look like a poor tramp colored, a man on the run all the time, what is it you done with all that money you say you stole? Believe I'd want to at least git me a new pair of shoes, mebbe a second shirt. How we know you ain't jist lyin'?"

Bass smiled and nodded. "'At's a dang good question, Miz Cuder. I kin see yo' point. But the po'er I looks, the mo' invisible I becomes. Lookin' like this, I kin walk down the main street of a town, ain't nobody sees me. A fancied-up colored man, even a little bit, worries a white man.

"Nah, I gots me a hideout where I stashes all my spoils. Someday, when I gets enough hay in the barn, I'm gone quit all this outlawin' and go on down to N'Ahlins, mebbe open me up a ho' house. Plenty of rich-lookin' black men down there ain't perturbin' nobody."

"You got a hideout?" Dooley asked, clearly impressed.

"Why sho' I do," Jonesy said. "Ever' outlaw worth his salt gots a hideout."

Truman rubbed his grimy stubbled chin, thoughtful, as he listened to all this. "You reckon we could join up and go rob us a bank sum'ers?"

"'Spects so," Jonesy replied. "We could go over there tomorruh. Get up early and takes yo' mules, could be there by noon. Need t'run by my hideout first t'get some things."

*This is going better than I thought*, Bass said to himself. Didn't look like he was going to need the handcuffs after all.

"Wish *we* had a hideout," Dooley said wistfully.

They'd gotten up well before dawn, Ma Cuder already had breakfast cooking. She had mixed emotions about the boys going off with Mister Smith. On the one hand she felt he could teach the idjits a thing or two; that is, if'n he's what he said. She had a nagging doubt, though; something about Jonesy Smith just didn't sit right with her. Of course, she also didn't much want the boys to be gone again, not liking one dang bit having to attend to all that hog farmin' by herself.

"You boys better damn sure get all your chores done afore you taken off. Ain't right you leavin' me here to do all the work," she groused.

Out in the hog shed Dooley poured the corncob and fish-gut slurry into the hog trough while Truman mixed it with a hoe, and the pigs crowded in to get their share. "I been thinkin'," Dooley said.

"I seriously doubt that," his brother responded.

Dooley ignored the derision. "If'n that Jonesy taken us to his hideout, we could look to rob him instead of no bank."

Truman stopped his mixing and leaned on the hoe handle, suddenly astounded at his idjit brother's insight. After a bit, he smiled and said, "Why hell yeah, we could.

If'n he's got all that robbin' loot stashed there, like he says, we could kill him and take it ourselves. Wouldn't nobody know nothin' about it, neither. Dang, Dooley, you's one of them gotdamn idjit geniuses I heard about."

Dooley grinned and nodded, poured slop. Hawed with pleasure that his older brother gave him some credit.

They'd saddled up and headed out not long after sunrise, Bass on one mule, the brothers on the other. Truman had Pete's Peacemaker wedged in his pants, Dooley the dragoon.

Three miles out, Truman called out. His and Dooley's mule clopped along two lengths behind Bass's. "How fer to your hideout, Jonesy?" he asked.

"'Bout a half day's ride," Reeves answered. "Need to meet up with some fellers along the way."

"What fellers?" Dooley asked. "Them your gang?"

"Guess you could say that," Bass said.

"Why we need to meet up with 'em?" Truman asked. "I thought it uz jist gonna be us three does that bank."

"Yeh, that's right. I just needs t'take sumpin to them boys first," Bass said.

"Take 'em whut?" Dooley wanted to know.

"Info'mation on the where-abouts of some desperados. Some of them boys is bounty hunters."

Truman stood in the stirrups. "Bounty hunters?" He shouted. "You ride with bounty hunters?"

"Well, sure I does. They ain't a whole lot of difference between bounty huntin' and outlawin'. All gotta make a livin' somehow."

"How come they don't take you in for the bounty? How we know they won't take us in?"

"We got us an understandin'. They helps me, I helps them. You boys got a bounty on yo' head?"

"Don't reckon. Ain't heard of none such."

"Well, then you ain't got nothin' to worry about."

Near noon Bass recognized the terrain as being near where his outfit had camped. He knew his boys would hear them coming, and not seeing Bass, have their guns drawn. That's what the deputy wanted, so he needed to get behind the Cuders and their mule before they rode into camp.

"I needs to stop here and take a piss," Reeves said. "You boys can ride on. I'll ketch up with ya."

Truman nodded. The road approached a rise. Truman made a clicking sound with his mouth and boot-heeled the mule in the flanks to keep it walking. Bass did his business and re-mounted, following the Cuders. Trotted his mule up to about ten yards behind the other mule just before they topped the rise.

Some thirty yards in front of them they could see the campsite with a curl of smoke coming from a cook fire. All the men there looked up at the approaching riders, three men standing, three sitting beside one of the wagons. Two of the standing men drew out their pistols, hung them loosely at their sides; the other, near what looked like a cook wagon, picked up a leaning shotgun.

"Them your boys, Jonesy?" Truman asked.

"Yep, that's them," Bass replied.

"Don't look none too friendly," Dooley said.

Truman stopped his mule and peered at the group. "Reckon you'd better git up here and introduce us, Jonesy, afore one of 'em decides to shoot us."

The Cuder brothers heard behind them the distinct sound of a hammer being eared back on a Colt. "You two boys need to put your hands straight up," said Jonesy. "Either of you starts to reach for your gun, I'll shoot you, and so will my men."

The brothers watched as Jud and Willie started walking towards them, their drawn pistols raised to point at their chests. The Cuders did as they were told. "What's goin' on here?" Truman asked.

"Boys, I'm Deputy Marshal Bass Reeves, and you're under arrest for stealing the U.S. Mail among other things. We're taking you back to Fort Smith to stand trial."

"Well, I'll be damned," Truman said.

"This mean we ain't going to your hideout?" Dooley whined.

Sitting in the prisoner wagon chained to the others, Truman looked around him as the wagon trundled along. "You boys outlaws, too?" he asked.

Lefty Shoemaker and Mannford Sizemore looked at Truman, then each other. Buffalo Jake stayed balled up in a corner, his buffalo-robed back to them, presumably asleep. "Aw, hell no," Lefty said. "Me and Sizemore here is nuns." He gestured toward the hairy hulk at the front of the wagon bed. "That there's a grizzly bear."

Truman nodded back. Buffalo Jake coughed and snuffled and moved around a bit. Dooley stared wide-eyed at the furry mound, scooted a little closer to his brother. A four-foot length by two-inch diameter piece of post oak windfall lay in the middle of the wagon bed. Dooley picked it up, and held it like a spear.

"How come it is you none's has been took in by the law?" Truman inquired. "What exactly you mean when you say you's none's?"

Lefty grinned. "You mean you ain't never seen a nun?"

"Well, reckon I have if'n they's to look like you. If by none, you mean your left arm, which you ain't got none."

Lefty and Mannford howled. Lefty slapped his right knee over and over with his one hand.

Jake rolled over, half rose up. "AAAUURUUCK!" he bellowed. Lefty and Mannford got immediately silent. Jake laid back down, re-adjusting the robe, again with his back to the others.

"What t'hell *is* that?" Dooley asked, his voice quivering a bit.

Mannford put his finger to his lips. "That's Buffalo Jake," he whispered. "Best not make any noise when he's sleepin'."

They rolled along through the slow rocking miles, the only sounds coming from the creak of the wagon, the rattle of the traces, the occasional blow of a horse. None of the prisoners or riders talked.

Truman kept staring at the massive buffalo hide hump hiding the giant creature underneath it. "That thing ain't moved in hours," he said. "I think it's dead." He took the four-foot tree limb from his brother's hand, poked the matted fur of the robe.

"I wouldn't do that, if'n I's you," Lefty said.

"I believe that thing's dead," Truman repeated, gave Jake's back another couple jabs.

"Smells dead," Dooley offered.

The hump stirred, started to rise. The hairy, angry visage of Jake turned toward Truman, his small eyes blazing out of the facial underbrush like fire coals. Jake woofed like a bear, and lunged at his stick-holding tormentor, his massive hand clamping around Truman's neck like the chomp of a timber wolf's jaw.

Lifting Truman up off the wagon bed, Jake held him at arm's length and watched him kick and struggle and turn blue. Truman swung the oak limb he still held as hard as he could, striking Jake across his left ear. Jake growled, grabbed Truman's club-wielding upper arm and snapped it like a twig. Truman tried to howl in anguish, but no air could escape his constricted throat.

Dooley stood, kicked Jake as hard as he could between the legs. The giant said, "Hummph," and dropped Truman. Instead of curling up in pain, as Dooley expected, Jake turned and looked down at the other Cuder. Jake knocked Dooley down with a back-handed forearm to the chest. He grabbed an ankle in each hand, raised the legs and spread them. With the force of a bull buffalo, Jake stomped his big boot into Dooley's crotch.

Just as Jake took Dooley's right leg into the clutch of both his arms with the intent to render it unusable, the butt of Deputy Reeve's Henry slammed into the base of his skull. Jake staggered, but didn't go down. He turned to look at his newest assailant, so Bass gave him another rifle stock butt-bash to the forehead. Jake's head snapped back some, he gave the Deputy sort of a quizzical look, his eyes crossed and he went to his knees. Toppled forward like a felled oak, hitting the wagon bed face-first with a whump.

Bass looked past the carcass of Buffalo Jake at the carnage. Dooley had curled himself into a ball, clutching his damaged parts, gasping out swear words with a distinct squeak in his voice. Truman lay at one side of the wagon alternately coughing and sobbing, his right arm bent unnaturally and useless at his side. The other two prisoners had scuttled as far to the tail-end of the wagon as their chains would allow, their pale expressions terror-stricken.

"Damn," Lefty said.

Bass had diverted their course up to Tishomingo where he knew a doc could patch up his wounded. Didn't figure any of them would die, but he thought he'd better get them checked out, and something needed to be done with Truman's arm. Thought he'd kilt Jake; turned out he'd only knocked him cold for a while. Dang ol' buffalo skinner just too thick-headed and mean to kill. Still, it aggravated him to have to make the turn and stopover at Tishomingo. Not only did it delay their return to Fort Smith, but it cost him twenty dollars in medical bills, for which he would not be reimbursed. It would all cut into his fees and reward money.

Back on the trail, reflecting on all this, Bass said to his posseman Jud riding next to him, "Them damn Cuder brothers has got to be the stupidest outlaws we ever brung in."

"Believe that t'be true enough," Jud responded.

"I just hope we can keep them alive long enough to collect the reward," Bass said.

**Editor's Note:** This story first appeared in the Western short story anthology, *Dead or Alive,* published by La Frontera Publishing in June 2013.

# Last Will for an Outlaw

*They was plenty times Bass was shot at during his deputying years, but no bullet ever found him. He's shot through the hat, through his coat, oncest a slug even knocked a button off'n his vest, but ain't narry a one even scratched him. Bass stood taller'n most men. He's brave enough in his own right, but did seem to have uh angel lookin over his shoulder. No sir, I ain't never knowed a man more respected for his guts and honor than Deputy Marshal Bass Reeves, by lawman and outlaw alike. – Posseman Jud Coldstone*

Jim Webb rode with fury, because he was plenty pissed. That old nigruh preacher had set a fire that'd burned more than a hundred acres of pasture off the ranch Webb bossed, the Washington-McLish spread out west of Ardmore. Preacher Steward's small outfit butted up against it. Webb decided he'd ride over, have done with it once and for all.

Webb was not a calm man, nor a gentle one. Up from Texas, Billy Washington had hired him on as foreman for his vast cattle ranch in the Chickasaw Nation. He drifted in one day looking for cow work. Billy's partner, Dick McLish, knew of Webb, had heard he'd killed a dozen men. Billy found it hard to distinguish from appearances whether the man was a cowman, or a common outlaw. You could tell he's a tough, mean, and hardnosed sumbitch, probably even cold-blooded. Thing was, though, with the rough-edged hands they already had, with rustlers and outlaws already overflowing the Territory, Webb was just the kind of man they needed for the top boss job.

Webb saw two people outside the cabin as he rode up. One, a man in is late fifties with salt and pepper hair, the other a boy, maybe fifteen, both black. They were digging postholes, building a hog pen. The pair paused in their work to watch him approach.

The preacher looked concerned, apprehensive, as did the boy. Webb's reputation swung wide. Still, the preacher tried to be cordial. Pulled a bandana from a hip pocket, wiped his face. "Mornin', Mistah Webb," he said.

Webb ignored the greeting. Reining up his sorrel five yards from the preacher, he leaned forward on the saddle horn. "You burnt off a hunnert acres of my grazin' pasture, Steward."

The old man put his bandana back in his pocket, and shoved his posthole digger back into the fresh hole, leaning his forearm on the handle tops. "Well, it was uh accident, Mistah Webb. I's burnin' off some brush an' the wind come up, carried them sparks out int' thet grass. I tried to whop it all out, but it jest got plum away from me.

"It was a mistake on my part, I admit. Look here, what you reckon's the damages. I pay you for it, if I can. Mebbe give you some uh my beeves."

Webb had dismounted by then coming right up to the preacher's face. "Hell, if I took your whole herd, it wouldn't be enough. 'Sides, I couldn't feed 'em nohow with all that grass burnt off. Can't even graze my own head, you igernant black bastard!"

The preacher's expression got hard. "Now hold on there, Webb. Ain't no call to start name callin'. Tole you I'd make repairs. Tole you it was uh accident."

"Accident, my ass!" Webb's fury built. "You need to pack up and git off'n this land, you dumb nigger!" He put a hand on the preacher's chest, gave him a shove.

The boy pulled up the steel rod he held and advanced toward Webb, his eyes burning. Webb saw him and threw out his Colt, cocked back the hammer and pointed it between the teenager's eyes.

"What you think you gonna do, boy?" Webb demanded. "You come any closer with that tampin' arn and I'll blow yer damn head off."

The preacher put his hand out toward the boy. "You stay right there, James," he said to him. He returned his hard stare to Webb.

"Webb, you tell Mistah Washington I be over there tomarrah an' we work this out. Right now, I think it best you git on off my land. I's through talkin' to you."

Webb uncocked his pistol and turned back to Steward. "I reckon I'm through talkin' to you, too."

He whacked the preacher across his left ear with the pistol barrel. The man staggered, but didn't go down. Webb whacked him again. Steward crumpled to his knees, and Webb hit him with the pistol on the crown of his head. The preacher fell face-down onto the ground. Webb started kicking him in the head and ribs, over and over. The boy leapt, falling across the preacher's body to protect him.

"Stop it!" he hollered. "You're killin' him!"

Webb kicked the boy.

The black man and the boy lay still on the ground, Steward's head and face bloody. The boy bled from the nose and scalp. Webb, breathing heavily, holstered his gun, mounted up, and rode off.

From a 1914 newspaper interview with Jud Coldstone, former posseman and guard for Deputy U.S. Marshals out of the Federal Court in Fort Smith, Arkansas, presided over by Judge Isaac Parker:

*In the Spring of '83 we struck out from Judge Parker's Court in Fort Smith for the Chickasaw Nation to arrest a man named Jim Webb. The warrant for him said he'd kilt a man in cold blood, plum beat him to death.*

*Gener'ly speakin', deputies would gather up a batch of writs, then hire on a posseman or two and a cook. They'd all head out to the Ter'tory to round up the outlaws. Most times them trips out and back would take three, four weeks, sometimes as long as two months, dependin' on how long it tuck to chase some uh them boys down, and, uh course, the weather.*

*Believe I'd come to be Bass Reeves's favorite posseman. You see, I could read and write, which Bass could not do—him havin' growed up a slave and all—and he liked to take me along to help him sort out all his writs, so's he could serve the right one on whoever he was arrestin' at the time. He come to trust me more'n others on this, believin' I'd hand him the right writ to serve. Also like to think he 'preciated how I handled myself in tight sit'chashuns, which we had some. 'Course, I bein' mostly Creek Indin prolly helped our association, as he had run away from down in Texas, had come up to live with the people during the States War. We both spoke that Muscogee tongue. And, a course, we was friends.*

He picked up a blue chip—the last one he had—rolling it through his fingers, mulled over what to do. The bet was to him, but couldn't decide if his pair of tens would be worth the two-bits of his call. Before he could choose, the big lawman entered the saloon. Busted through the door and clomped over to the table where the card players sat.

"I got a warrant, Jud," he said without preamble. "We best git goin'."

Jud Coldstone looked up at the tall black man staring down at him. The deputy looked more somber than usual, his thick black mustache adding to his severe visage. Something about that told Jud he'd best not hesitate in following the deputy, who had turned and started back out the door. Jud tossed his cards onto the table and frowned. "Guess I'm out, boys."

Jud caught up with Reeves down the street. Had to trot to catch up, as the big man's stride was purposeful and long.

"Who you want me to fetch, Bass?" Coldstone asked, coming up next to the deputy. "You want just Edgar and Bill, or should I get more?"

"Don't need an outfit this time. Jest be you 'n me," Reeves answered.

Coldstone scampered alongside the deputy, thinking over what had just been told him. "Wull, how many writs you got? You think just the two of us can handle 'em?"

"Got just one, Jud. We taken off for west of Tishomingo. Goin' after a man kilt a friend of mine."

"Chickasaw land? And you don't want to take Bill along? That's a powerful long way out, Bass. None too friendly country, neither. Who's gonna do our cookin'?" Jud's question trailed down to a despaired whine, he already figured he knew the answer.

"We'll take hardtack and beans. Do our own cookin'. Figure we can scare up a jack rabbit or two along the way. We need to ride hard."

"I'uz afeared you'd say that," Jud muttered.

They'd been told Jim Webb was at a line house out on the range. "Ride southwest out of Ardmore," they'd been told, "along the Arbuckles, out about twenty miles. Sooner or later you'll spot it. It's the only cabin out there."

Reeves could see a string of white smoke curling up into the red dawn sky, and pulled up his bay. "That must be it," he said to his partner.

Two log buildings sat in a wide valley, one twice as big as the other separated by a twenty-foot dog run. The ribbon of smoke issued from a tin stovepipe sticking out of the roof of the smaller structure.

Reeves' didn't plan to ride in and announce himself. With a man like Webb, that'd only get him and Jud shot. They'd have to make Webb think they's just a couple of cowboys passing through. That's why he rode the bay out of Fort Smith instead of the black. It'd been a dead give-a-way if he had. No wandering cowboy rode a black stallion.

"We'll ride in there and ask 'em for breakfast," Bass said. "Tell 'em we come off a drive and is headed back to Texas. While we's eating, we'll figure the best way to arrest Webb. Hopefully, there won't be no gunplay."

Reeves and Coldstone spurred their horses into a trot headed toward the log houses. Two men stood outside the door of the bigger cabin, watching them. One was tall and lean, the other stocky and thick. Both drew their pistols, holding them at their sides.

"Mornin'," Bass said when they came up to the men. "Wonderin' if'n we could get some breakfast."

"Who're you boys?" the stocky one asked, none too hospitable. He's big but not tall, thick at the chest and shoulders; had an unshaven hard look. Reeves figured him to be Webb.

"Just passin' through," Reeves said, taking off his hat and wiping brow sweat with his forearm. "We come off a drive up to Dodge. Headed back to Gainesvull."

"What outfit?"

"The Four Sixes, Burk Burnett," Bass answered.

The big man thought about that, slapping the barrel of his gun against his pant leg, thinking. "You still ain't told me your names," he said.

"I'm Dusty Jones," Bass said. "This here's Jud Coldstone." Grinned back at the man. "And who might you be, mister?" he asked.

"Name's Webb," the man said. He gestured with his pistol toward the other. "Frank Smith."

"You Jim Webb?" Bass asked.

"That's right," came the answer.

“Well, I heard uh you,” Reeves said, grinning big and shaking his head. “Yessuh, I surely have.” His comment seemed to displease the man.

“You go on in the cook house there and tell ole Abner what you want.” Webb indicated the small cabin.

“Well, thank ya kindly, Mistuh Webb.” Reeves and Jud dismounted.

“Jud, you go on in there and tell the cook I’d like some eggs and biscuits,” Reeves said. He turned to Webb. “You wouldn’t mind if I watered the horses, would ya? Maybe give ’em some feed?”

Webb looked annoyed. “Take ’em on out to the stable,” he said.

As Reeves led the two horses, Webb followed behind. Bass snuck a glance back, saw Webb still held his pistol at his side. The animals stopped at the trough and drank while Reeves loosened the saddle cinches.

“Yessuh, Jim Webb. I shore nuf heard uh that name,” he said laughing and smiling.

“What is it you heard?” Webb asked, still not smiling.

“Well, that you a top boss ain’t to be trifled with. That you about the toughest man around, mebbe the meanest.”

“Hmph,” Webb responded, nodding.

Reeves reached up and removed his Winchester from its saddle boot. Webb tensed, raise his gun some. Holding the rifle by the barrel, Bass leaned it against the stable wall, and fetched a bucket of feed, pouring it into the trough.

“Also heard said you’s killed some men.” Bass set down the bucket and looked Webb square in the eye, his smile gone. Both men stared at each other for several long seconds, neither speaking. The horses moved to the feed trough and started to eat.

Reeves patted the neck of the bay. “Well, I ’spect them eggs is ready,” he said picking up his rifle by the barrel and slinging it under his arm.

Bass and Jud took up seats at the table in the small cook house and started in on their breakfasts. Webb and the man Smith stayed outside, standing in the dog run, talking earnestly to one another in low tones, glancing now and then into where the two men sat eating. The cook picked up a metal bucket and left the kitchen.

“I ain’t so sure they’s believin’ our story,” Reeves said. Jud looked out at them, then back at his plate.

Reeves continued, not looking up. “We need to make our move quick. After we finish up here, we’ll go sit on that bench outside the door. Roll us up a smoke, act like ain’t nothin’ goin’ on. You sit at one end, me t’other. I figure Webb will stay with me. When the time’s right and they’s off guard, I’ll give you a sign. You get Smith’s gun away from him, I’ll take care of Webb.”

“Awright,” Jud said, grabbing up his coffee cup and taking a sip.

Reeves sat down on the split oak bench, and pulled makings out of his shirt pocket. “Now that was a damn fine breakfast,” he said. Jud took his place at the other end of the bench. Just as Reeves had thought, Webb had come up to stand beside him, his pistol still in hand. Bass had to be careful what he said, how he acted.

“You boys need to ride on out of here,” Webb said.

"Well, we'll do that, Mistuh Webb. Don't mean to overstay our welcome. Just thought we'd have a smoke first afore we head out. That okay with you?"

Webb just looked at him.

"Nosuh," Bass continued congenially. "I can't hardly eat a meal like that without relaxin' with a smoke afterward. Didn't get much chance fo' that out on the trail; didn't get that good a cookin' neither. You got a fine cook here, Mistuh Webb, yessuh."

Reeves could tell Webb was getting agitated. The man kept tapping the barrel of his gun against his thigh, which he held in his left hand. If something didn't happen pretty quick, Bass was certain Webb and his cohort would just up and shoot them. But Webb never took his eyes off Bass, Reeves knew he'd get shot if he made a move. Couldn't signal Jud, neither, as long as Webb kept staring at him.

Reeves kept rolling his smoke, kept yammering about this and that, whatever came to mind. He glanced over at Jud; looked like his pard was about to fall asleep. Even if he did signal him, he'd probably miss it.

The cook came around the corner of the cook house and clanged the water-filled bucket he carried against a metal tub at the side of the cabin, pouring the water into it. Webb jumped, turned to look toward the noise. In that instant, Reeves decided to act, but didn't have time to signal Jud.

He leapt up clutching Webb's throat in his left hand, at the same time, his right latched onto the man's gun hand. Slammed Webb up against the rough log wall of the cabin banging his gun hand hard against it until Webb dropped the pistol. Reeves squeezed the big fingers of his powerful left hand tighter around Webb's neck until the man began to sputter and turn red, his eyes bulging.

Jud froze at the commotion, momentarily unsure what to do. Smith raised his pistol and fired at Reeves. A piece of the log wall above Bass's head splintered. Smith fired again and the slug clipped the rim of Reeve's hat, knocking it off his head.

Rattler quick, Bass drew out his Colt with his right hand and swung around sideways, pointing the pistol back behind him. Still clinching Webb's neck with his left hand, he fired one shot hitting Smith in the midsection.

The force of the .44 slug knocked the cowboy backwards off his feet causing him to expel air with a "Hoomph!" His gun left his grip as he fell. On the ground Smith felt at the bullet hole in his belly. "Gawd awmighty," he said.

"Dammit, Jud," Reeves said to his partner.

Now alert, Jud had drawn out his gun and stood over Smith, pointing it at him. "Sorry, Bass. You surprised me."

Webb flailed at his big assailant with his fists. Turning back to him, Reeves tightened his grip some more on his prisoner's throat, shoved the business end of his Colt hard up against Webb's left nostril.

"I ain't agin blowin' your brains out, Webb. That preacher you kilt was a friend of mine. This writ I got says I can bring you back dead or alive, so it don't much matter to me."

Webb slumped, giving up his fight, and Reeves released his choke hold. Webb bent at the waist coughing and gasping for air.

"Git over here and cuff up this sumbitch, Jud," Reeves said.

*We taken a wagon that day, which was there at the line house, to haul our prisoners back to Fort Smith. Bass told that old negro cook, Abner, to go back to Mister Washington and tell him about what had happened to his foreman and cowhand. To also tell Mister Washington we had took his wagon and two horses—those belonging to Webb and Smith—to transport our prisoners. And that if he wanted to recover them, he could do so at the U.S. District Court in Fort Smith.*

*That Smith fella, bein' gut shot like he was, lasted until the morning of the second day before he expired. We wasn't but a half day out of Tishomingo in the Chickasaw Nation, so we hauled him on in to there and had him buried in a outlaw's grave. Bass told the undertaker to send a bill to the court for the pine box and grave diggin', and we continued on for Fort Smith with Webb still in tow.*

*Bass collected the fees for bringin' Webb in, but I think he was more satisfied to bring him to justice for killin' that preacher friend of his than he was for the money. That's why he was plenty dang galled when someone talked a court commissioner into settin' bail for Webb, and he got out. However, as expected, Webb's trial date came and went without him showin' up. So Bass got his new warrant, and we headed out again to fetch him back. We hooked up with Deputy Jim Mershon as he had several writs of his own and allowed as how he would need Bass's help on some. Bass went along with it, but the onliest arrest he had in mind to make was Jim Webb's.*

*Word had it that Webb had drifted back to the Chickasaw land, and was saw hanging out at a general store owned by a whiskey runner named Jake Bywater, the man who'd put up his bail. The store was located on the south side of the Arbuckles where the Whiskey Trail went up into them mountains.*

Bass reined up the black, and pointed at a wooden sign stuck on a single post. "What's that sign read, Jud?" he asked. It had a red arrow pointing up the trail with some words, also painted in red, next to it.

"It says 'Bywater Store,'" Coldstone answered.

Reeves turned in his saddle studying the lay of the land. The trail cut through a thick stand of woods, but he could see part of a clearing up ahead where the road curved, and beyond that the edge of a corn field.

"Store must be around that bend," Bass said. "I'm going to cut in through these woods and approach it from there. We go riding right up plain as day, and Webb's in that store, he's gonna hightail it.

"You ride on up the trail and go into the store. Webb ain't going to be expecting you. I'll wait at the edge of these woods. You spot him in there, you signal me by coming back outside and taking your hat off. I see that I'll come riding up quick. Maybe we can catch him off guard and arrest him afore any trouble starts."

Jud walked through the open door and paused. The light shift to near-dark inside the store momentarily blinded him. Two windows stood un-shuttered, open to let in sunlight and air, one on the side wall to his left, the other at the front of the store to his right. Place smelled of stale tobacco and corn and unwashed bodies with a mix of pickle brine thrown in. Jud chanced a quick look around, keeping his chin down. Dared not raise his head too much, figuring all eyes inside had turned to him, including Webb's if he's in there. Most likely, Webb would not recognize him, but it didn't hurt to be cautious. He counted four men in the place; two seated at one table, one at another.

A long counter ran along the front of the back wall. A fat man stood behind it, leaning on his hands splayed flat on the two by twelve rough cedar bartop, watching Jud. Coldstone walked toward him.

The posseman put his elbows on the counter, leaning forward. "You got any whiskey?" he asked.

"This here's Indin Territory," the fat man said in a gruff voice. "Spirits is agin the law." He had a greasy, pinched face covered with a five-day gray stubble, and wore red long handles under bib overalls, neither of which looked to have ever seen a wash tub for some time. His expression didn't invite friendship.

Jud grinned and took a quick, furtive look around the room. Thought the man at a table by the front window could be Webb, but he'd have to have a closer look. Turning back to the fat man he said, "Well, I reckon that'd be the right answer, if'n I's the law. Now what do you got?"

"Best I can offer is some of my own brewed beer. It ain't got spirits. Ten cents a glass."

Jud gave out a low whistle. "Must be some damn good brew at that price," he said and grinned at the proprietor again. The man stared back at him.

"Well, I reckon I'll just go git me a drink backit that crik I rode past," Jud said.

The fat man crossed his arms at his chest looking at Jud darkly. The posseman turned and headed for the door, still keeping his head bowed. Glanced up as he got closer to the man sitting at the window, who looked back at him intently. By God, it damn sure was Webb. The posseman lowered his hat brim and walked out the door. Once on the porch he removed his hat and wiped his brow.

Reeves spurred the stallion hard, they broke from the trees covering the hundred yards of open ground to the store at a full gallop.

Webb had watched the skinny little man from the minute he'd entered. Had to be suspicious of strangers out in these parts. Had to figure they was either whiskey runners, renegades, or lawmen. The man who'd stepped through the door looked like he could be any one of those, they was something about him looked familiar. It made Webb uneasy. Generally speaking, whiskey runners and renegades didn't make him uneasy.

When the fella stepped out onto the store porch and took off his hat, it hit Webb—that was the posseman from the last time he'd run into Bass Reeves, and that's who he saw galloping toward him.

Grabbing his Winchester leaning against the wall, Webb stood and ran across the room leaping head first out the open side window, hitting the ground in a roll. Quickly back on his feet, he started for the stable, but Reeves was headed that way to cut him off. Webb could tell he'd never make it to his horse. He turned and took out at a dead run toward the corn field about an eighth of a mile behind him. Reeves called out for him to stop, but he kept running.

At about a hundred yards, Webb started to give out. The concealment of the corn field still lay more than a hundred yards beyond him. Reeves hollered something again. Webb pulled up; decided he might as well shoot it out with the deputy in the open. Not likely he'd make the cover of the corn, anyway, and didn't want to go down without a fight. Breathing hard, he swung around and levered a round into the Winchester's firing chamber, raising it to his shoulder. His breathing still labored, took as careful aim as he could, sighted down the barrel and squeezed the trigger.

Reeves saw the man leap from the window and guessed it was Webb, figured h's running to the stable to get his horse. He reined the black toward the structure and gave the animal another kick. Webb, seeing that, retreated toward the distant corn field behind him.

"You ain't getting' away, Webb!" Reeves called to the fugitive. "You best throw down your guns and give up!"

But the man didn't stop running.

"Webb!" Reeves called out again. "You know I'll shoot you!"

The man stopped and bent at the waist, putting his hands on his knees, still keeping his back toward the lawman. Reeves thought Webb was ready to give up, so parked the butt of his rifle onto his right thigh. Gripped it at the waist, his finger resting on the trigger guard, the barrel pointed skyward.

Webb turned to face him. "You the one's about to die, Reeves!" Webb hollered across the distance. Put his rifle to his shoulder and fired. The slug whanged off Reeve's saddle horn, and the stallion shuffled. Webb levered another round and fired again; the lapel of Reeves coat jumped out and a button flew off. A third shot cut the reins Reeves held in his left hand.

Webb's rifle jammed, and he threw it down. Started running straight at the deputy. Pulled his pistol and began firing it, yelling and cursing as he advanced. Reeves swung down off his horse and came to one knee just as a slug from Webb's pistol slapped into the ground one foot to his left. Levering a round, the deputy calmly leveled the rifle and fired. And levered again.

Webb jerked back and to his right, but didn't fall. Once more he came forward, screaming his defiance. Raised his pistol.

Reeves aimed and fired. Webb spun to his left and went hard to the ground, rolling onto his back, less than fifty yards from the deputy. Webb still held his pistol in his right hand. Reeves stood and waited, his rifle at the ready.

"You've kilt me, Reeves," Webb called out. "I need to see you afore I go."

"Toss that pistol away," Reeves hollered. Webb flung the weapon into the grass three feet away. The deputy walked up to him, his rifle still pointed at the dying man. Jud came running up followed by the store keeper and another man. They all stood looking down at Webb, watching him breathe his last, two bullet wounds in his chest.

"You're a brave man, Bass," Webb said. He coughed once, blood bubbling from his mouth and nose. Reeves didn't respond.

"I want to give you my Colt and scabbard," Webb wheezed. "I want you to take it. I've kilt eleven men with it, and I expected you'd be the twelfth. I think you should have it."

Reeves stood there not quite sure what to say. Webb raised his hand. “Take my hand, Bass,” he said.

Reeves complied.

“I ain’t never met another man like you, Reeves. Now, I want you to have my Colt.”

While still gripping Reeves’ hand, he looked over at the fat man. “Bywater, you heard my dyin’ words. I want you to write ’em down.”

Saying that, Webb rattled his last breath and died.

*We didn’t haul the carcass of Jim Webb back to Fort Smith. We’s a good ten days out, and a dead man starts to putrefy to high heaven in about three. But that storekeep, Bywater, attested to the shootin’, saying it was for sure Webb who’d been kilt. Deputy Mershon had rode up by then, and took their statements.*

*Newspapers later reported Mershon was the one shot Webb. Back in them days having a colored deputy arrest or shoot a white man, even one as no ’count as Webb, was highly frowned upon. Indins or Mex’kins was okay, but not a white man.*

*Sometime around aught five, years after Bass had shut hisself of deputyin’, a man who said he was a history writer asked Bass what he could tell him about Jim Webb. Ol’ Bass jist smiled and said, “Believe that was a Mexican outlaw I oncest brought to justice over in the Chickasaw Nation. Warrant said he’s wanted dead or alive, and I done it both ways.”*

*Bass opened a desk drawer and pulled out a revolver. “This here’s his Colt .44 he give me at the time,” he said.*

## A Personal Note from the Author

Thank you for taking time to read *West of the Dead Line*. If you enjoyed it, please consider telling your friends or posting a short review on Amazon. Word of mouth is an author's best friend and much appreciated.

Would you consider being in my Readers Group? As a member you'll receive periodic emails from me (no spam) about new releases, promotions, giveaways, blog posts, etc. No more than about twice a month. I would love to have you in the group. Please vist my website to sign-up and receive a free ebook:

http://www.philtrumanink.com

Thanks again – Phil Truman

# Novels by Phil Truman

Red Lands Outlaw: The Ballad of Henry Starr

In the last years of the tough and woolly land called Indian Territory, and the first of the new state of Oklahoma, the outlaw Henry Starr rides roughshod through the midst of it. A native son of "The Nations" he's more Scotch-Irish than Cherokee, but is scorned by both. He never really wanted to journey west of the law, yet fate seems to insist. He's falsely accused and arrested for horse-thieving at age sixteen, then sentenced to hang at nineteen by Judge Isaac Parker for the dubious killing of a deputy U.S. marshal, but he escapes the gallows on a technicality. Given that opportunity, the charming, handsome, mild-mannered Henry Starr spends the rest of his life becoming the most prolific bank robber the West has ever known.

GAME: an American Novel

Year in and year out the football powerhouse Hert City Trojans import a ringer to fuel their championship charge, but their luck is about to change. In the small backwater town of Tsalagee, first-year coach Donny Doyle knows the only way he can fulfill his promise to unseat the Hert City juggernaut, is to beat them at their own *GAME*. But in his own recruit, the mammoth and powerful, yet troubled and ominous Leotis McKinley, Doyle finds more than he bargained for. Truman's character-rich novel *GAME* spins an energetic tale around the intensity of small-town high school football in America. And yet, amid the fast-paced drive of the story, lies an account of the human spirit struggling through adversity and finding victory. Readers of any age or gender will feel the triumph, honor, and glory that comes from the... *GAME*.

TREASURE KILLS: Legends of Tsalagee

Legends from a small town come in many forms. Near Tsalagee, Oklahoma a monster lurks and an infamous 19th Century outlaw's booty lays hidden. When two renegade bikers ride into town looking to find the Lost Treasure of Belle Starr, local legends Hayward Yost and Socrates Ninekiller suspect the ruffians' involvement in the murder of a local farmer; a man rumored to have knowledge of the lost treasure's location...and its curse. As events unfold, others in the community are drawn into the hunt – a Wiccan who moves to town to pursue her New Age lifestyle; her bumbling, socially inept boyfriend women can't seem to resist; a young Iraqi War veteran home to heal his physical and emotional wounds; and a mysterious creature known in Native American lore as a forest demon whom they call "Hill Man who screams at night." Mystery, romance, comedy, and adventure await in *Legends of Tsalagee*.

Made in the USA
Monee, IL
02 February 2020

21206207R00120